Demon Hunters 2: Retribution

Demon Hunters 2
Retribution

Avril Sabine

Cracked Acorn Productions
Australia

Demon Hunters 2: Retribution

Published by

Cracked Acorn Productions

PO Box 1365

Gympie, Queensland 4570

Australia

978-1-925131-06-2 (Kindle)

978-1-925617-38-2 (EPUB)

978-1-925131-19-2 (Print)

Genre: Young Adult Urban Fantasy/Horror

Cover design by Caitlyn Petersen

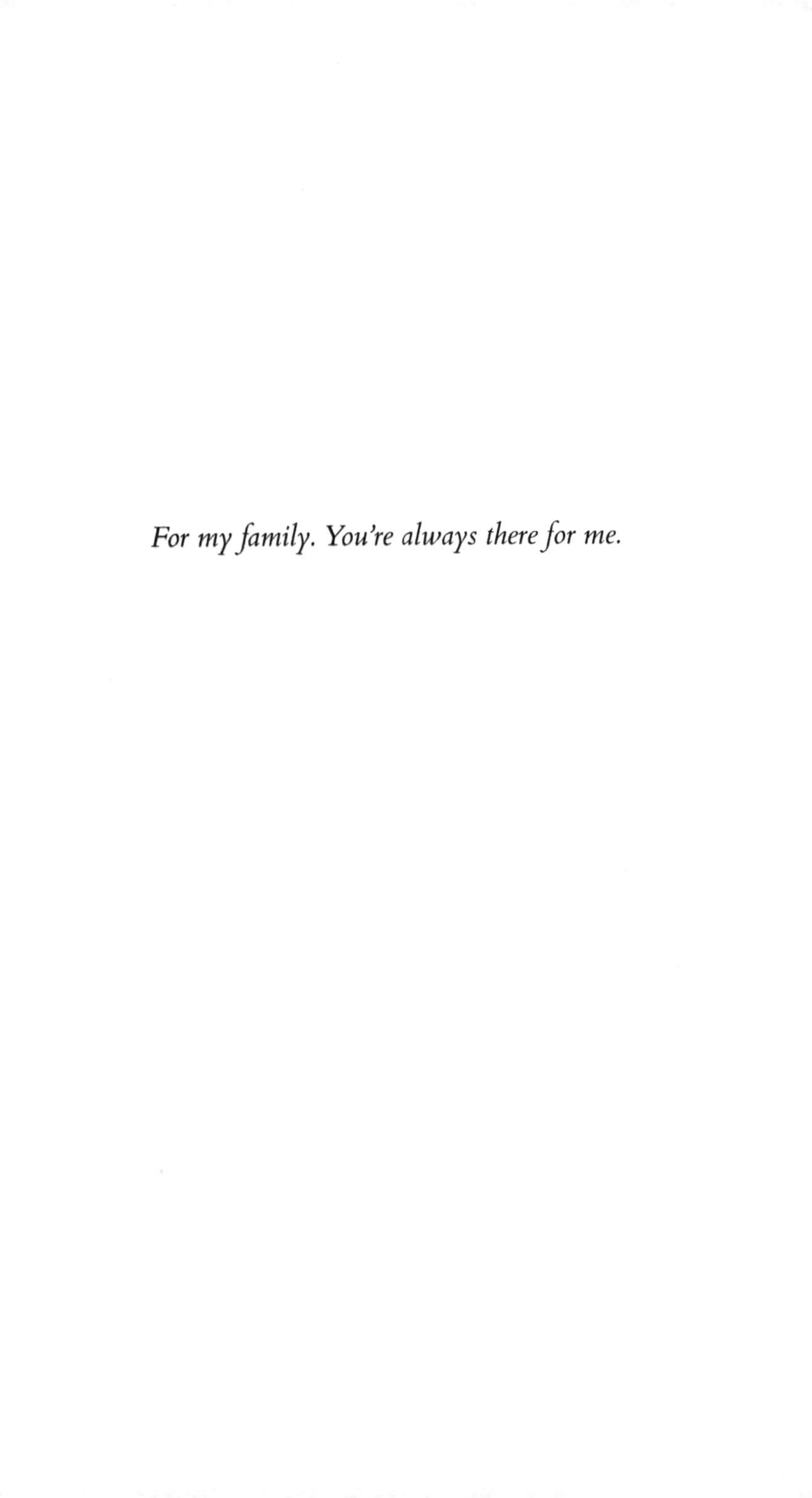

For my family. You're always there for me.

Scarlett knows the things that go bump in the night are real. Her family has hunted demons for generations. She has grown up learning how to banish them, seeing things most people couldn't imagine, even in their worst nightmares. In fact, hunting demons is just like many other jobs. The hours are long, the pay is nearly non-existent and the clients are determined to have their own way. Just like any other job… or at least it seemed that way before demons started hunting her.

*

This story was written by an Australian author using Australian spelling.

Chapter One

Scarlett Hunter glanced from the road to the scrawled directions her brother had given her. She frowned. Surely she should have reached the turnoff by now. Alex usually gave her clear directions, but she guessed he'd been in a hurry. She looked in the rear view mirror and seeing no one about, slowed down. This better not take too long. She didn't want to be stuck driving back into Brisbane during peak hour traffic.

She wasn't certain how she'd been talked into doing Alex's job. She only hoped Mrs Rose, the woman whose house she was looking for, wasn't in tears. She never knew how to comfort grieving people. They made her feel awkward. Give her a sword and a demon to face any day.

Scarlett glanced at the directions again and ran the fingers of one hand through her short blond hair that feathered around her face. With a shake of her head she stared at the deserted road. For all she knew, she was lost. Her cousin Riley would probably say she'd subconsciously got lost to get out of the job. She'd argue that comment. Anyone would've got lost with the directions she'd been given.

Scarlett checked the rear view mirror again, wondering if she should turn around and have another look in case she'd missed the turnoff. No, she'd drive a little further before doing that. She felt a tingle at her left wrist as a pop, more physical then audible, filled the car. Movement drew her gaze towards the passenger seat. Her breath caught in her throat, her body tensed and her mind whirled with a thousand questions as she tried to keep her attention on the road.

A young man now sat in the seat. He had light brown skin, dark wavy hair and eyes that could only be called black. And so beautiful it took all of her willpower to keep her eyes on the road.

"What–" Scarlett began. No. She wouldn't start talking to one of them. That wasn't what she'd been taught. Her jaw tightened on all the questions that wanted to spill forth.

Seeing a safe spot, she pulled over to the side of the road and turned the car off. As she jumped out, she tugged on the boot lever, pocketing her car keys.

Without a glance at her passenger she ran to the boot and pulled out a sword, unsheathing it.

Spinning around, she found the young man in front of her. She hadn't heard the door open, but that didn't surprise her. Holding the sword up, she took a step forward. The man held his ground. No surprise there, either.

"What do you want?" Scarlett met the dark eyes, distrust in her voice.

"Your help."

Now that was a surprise. Scarlett frowned. Maybe her assumption had been wrong. But what else could he be? "What are you?" Her words were cautious.

The man grinned wickedly. "I don't think you need to ask that question. You already know or you would not hold a blessed sword between us."

"Why would a demon ask a hunter for help? What trick are you up to?"

"I wish to cease to be."

Scarlett opened her mouth to speak. Her mind was blank. Surely she hadn't heard right. "You what?"

"Scarlett-"

When she heard him speak her name, fear rushed through her. Years of training was all that kept her calm. "I've never faced you before. How do you know me?"

"You're well known among my kind. I have a brother who talks of you often." He glanced at the narrow black line, with a hint of red in it, which snaked around her wrist. The line started at her pulse point in the middle of her wrist and travelled two and half times around her wrist to where it ended suddenly. A demon mark. It lengthened every time she sent a demon home.

"Then maybe your brother should stay in hell where he belongs." She knew demons didn't have the same meaning for brother as humans did. They were an ally or what passed for a friend amongst demons.

"Maybe your kind should stop calling him out of hell."

Scarlett inclined her head in acknowledgement of his words. "You still haven't told me what you want."

"But I have. You just chose not to believe me. I'm tired, Scarlett. Century after century spent at the beck and call of humans. I'm only a minor demon. Barely a sin at all."

"All major sins start with minor ones. Each step is that much closer than the last." Life would be much simpler if she could send demons to hell the moment she saw them. But the demons had to be causing harm or intending to. So far this demon was all talk, but with demons talk could be more dangerous than physical harm.

"Scarlett. I will be your doom unless you make me cease to be."

A warning or a threat? She couldn't be certain. Her eyes narrowed. Demons were tricky with words. Not to mention twisting what was said to them beyond recognition. "Prophecy? Clairvoyance? Or your own desire?"

"My desire is to be left in peace." He laughed abruptly. "I know, quite an oxymoron. A demon that desires peace. But your human dramas weary me. I would have an end to it."

Scarlett lowered her sword. You could only hold a sword aloft and in the one position for so long. Even when you trained almost daily, the weight became heavier the longer you held it. Her fingers went unconsciously to her throat to touch the gold cross that hung on a narrow leather necklace. "Why ask me?"

"My sin is not violence. It's lust." He leered at her to drive his point home.

Scarlett almost laughed. His antics reminding her of her cousin Riley. She caught herself in time. It was never a good idea to lower your defences around a demon. She glared at him. "What do you want, demon?" She stressed the last word to remind herself what it was she spoke to.

His lips curved into a smile. "Oh hunter, I could make you feel my sin if I wished. But it's your cooperation I need."

"Go away demon. I don't have time to stand here and talk in circles with you." Scarlett sheathed her sword and walked to the driver's side door, an eye on the demon the entire time. He hadn't done anything wrong yet, but that didn't make him trustworthy.

The moment she opened her door, he disappeared, reappearing in the passenger seat again. She sighed in frustration. Standing with her door open, she stared at the demon. He stared back, an unfathomable expression on his face.

"Great! Just what I need. A demon stalker. How lucky can I get?"

"I haven't started stalking you yet. The call to kill you hasn't been made."

"What?" Her heart leapt. She took a deep breath, reminding herself to remain calm. It should have been Alex on this lonely road, not her.

"Haven't you listened to a word I've said?"

"It'd help if you didn't talk in riddles and half sentences. Who will call you to kill me and why do you know about it when it hasn't happened? And you said doom. That doesn't have to mean death. Speak plainly, demon." Scarlett ran her fingers through her short hair, taking a deep breath. Patience, she reminded herself. And caution.

"I have hunter. I've asked for your help. I asked you to make me cease to exist before I'm called on to end your life. Ask me to seduce a woman and I'm yours. Ask me to torture someone until they beg for death and you need a different demon. I'm not a torturer. I know what'll happen to me if I fail. It'll be safer to no longer exist."

"Don't answer the call when it comes."

"It's not that simple."

"You demons always complicate things." How had she got to this point? Conversation with a demon. What next? Quit being a hunter? No way. She brushed her fingertips along the pommel of her sword. There had to be a way to simplify matters and get rid of him in a hurry. "Why can't you ignore the call?"

"I owe a powerful demon a favour. He can't answer the call even though he'd like to. You're the first stage of his revenge."

"What's this demon's name?"

"You don't know his true name. The name you'd recognise is Retribution."

The name echoed inside Scarlett's head and she shakily sat in the driver's seat. Retribution! She tucked her sword under the dash so the hilt rested on her seat and pulled out her phone. No coverage. She dropped it in her lap and leaned her head on the steering wheel, the demon beside her forgotten.

Retribution! The demon who'd lost a battle to her cousin Blake's girlfriend, Alyssa. It had been little more than a month now. She'd faced other demons since him. But none so powerful. With her head still down, Scarlett asked, "Why?"

"Because of the terms Alyssa set. Retribution's stuck in hell for a century."

Scarlett's head jerked up so she could look at him. "A century?" When he nodded, she sighed, leaned back in her seat and closed her eyes. "That's not possible. She didn't set out to do that." Her voice trailed off. "Completely impossible."

"She might not have planned to, but she's caused him to be bound to hell for a century."

Scarlett sighed. "I'm mad to even listen to you. Demons never tell the truth."

"Ask it of me."

Scarlett frowned and looked at him. "What?" It was hard to focus on what he said when the word 'doom' echoed in her mind. Doom and Retribution. Not a good combination. She forced herself to concentrate. You had to watch every little thing you said around a demon and every word they spoke or you'd end up in trouble.

"Ask truth of me and I can give you a binding oath to speak only truth for you."

"I will never ask a demon for anything. You lie, deceive and tempt. All you leave behind are broken minds and soulless bodies."

"Then I'll offer it to you for a token price."

"I have nothing I'm willing to give."

The demon slowly smiled, his eyes black pits of temptation. "Scarlett, I would ask so little of you. A kiss. What else would a demon of lust and desire require?" He reached out and ran his knuckle down her arm. His voice lowered. "A single kiss, Scarlett."

She pushed his hand away. "You're a demon!"

The demon laughed. His deep tone filled the car. "And you're a hunter."

"I won't kiss a demon!"

"I'm beginning to regret I must cease to exist. I've not been so entertained in ages."

"I don't have time to sit here and listen to your rubbish." She pushed the key into the ignition and turned it. As soon as she sorted out Mrs Rose's problem she'd go home to Gran. Hopefully she'd know what to do. She glanced at Alex's map and frowned. Where was the turn off?

"Another five kilometres."

Scarlett stared at the demon. She tried to ignore his looks, but she was only human. In her mind, she began to recite prayers. "How do you know what I was thinking?"

"Why bother asking questions when you won't trust in the answers?"

Scarlett's lips pressed tight together. She buckled her seat belt, slid her phone into her pocket, checked her mirrors and pulled onto the empty road. Five kilometres later she turned onto a rutted dirt road. She drove slowly and watched for the large red mailbox she'd been told sat by the driveway. And there it was, about four hundred metres along on her right.

She pulled up in front of the old timber cottage that was badly in need of paint. It had a verandah across the front, slightly sagging on one end. To one side of the door was a pile of boxes and on the other were two cane chairs with a wrought iron table between them.

"What's your name, demon?"

"I'm no fool. Give a hunter my true name? You may call me Desire." He smiled as she continued to glare at him.

"I won't be calling you anything then. Leave demon. You're not needed here."

"Demons are never needed, only wanted when someone needs their dirty work done."

"You're a demon. Don't expect me to feel sympathy for you." Scarlett opened the car door and her hand hovered over her sword. She couldn't take it with her even though every instinct screamed at her to remain armed. Her fingers curled into a fist and she turned away, closing the door with her other hand before she strode to the verandah. The demon walked beside her. She refused to acknowledge him and instead knocked on the front door.

Chapter Two

Within minutes the door swung open. A woman in her sixties with short steel-grey hair and metal-framed glasses stood there. She looked at Scarlett, with a single glance towards the demon. "Father Joe said he'd be sending a boy. Why are you here, girl?"

Scarlett took a calming breath and ignored the irritation in the woman's voice. She tried to tell herself it was preferable to tears. "I'm Scarlett." She gestured towards the boxes. "Are these the boxes you need taken to Father Joe… ahh…" For a moment she couldn't think of the woman's name, most of her attention was on the demon beside her. "Mrs Rose?"

"Who is he?" The woman stared at the demon.

Scarlett turned her gaze to him. He smiled lazily at her and didn't bother to introduce himself. He could have made himself invisible instead of making this job more difficult for her. Scarlett took another deep breath. She did the only thing she could. She shortened the name he'd offered her. "Des."

"Those are the boxes. All eight of them have to go. You got room in your car?"

Scarlett looked at the boxes and nodded her head. She took a couple of steps closer and reached out to pick up the first cardboard box. Before her fingers came in contact, her demon mark heated and she pulled her hands back as if something had bitten her.

Mrs Rose laughed bitterly. "You feel it too. My daughter said I was mad. Said I should sell the stuff. But I couldn't. Father Joe said he'd deal with it. I don't know what my brother was into, but you can rest assured he isn't with the angels in heaven. I'm betting he's warming his toes at the fires of hell."

"Where did you find these things?" Scarlett looked past Mrs Rose to stare at the house.

"Not in there. A little timber shed out the back. I'm going to burn it to the ground. Makes me feel like I'm being watched every time I go near it." Mrs Rose shuddered.

"Can I see it?"

"Around the back. You can't miss it. I keep expecting to see gargoyles perched on the ridge. But you won't get me near it anymore than I have to."

"Thank you." Scarlett hesitated only a moment

before she strode back to the car. With one demon already shadowing her she wasn't about to take any unnecessary chances. Mrs Rose could think what she wanted. She dropped the belt of her sword over her head and one arm, so it rested against her back. Picking up a second vial of holy water, she slid it into her pocket next to the one already in there. The vial was about the size of her little finger, but she wouldn't need much. A drop of holy water went a long way when dealing with demons.

"You'd be better off taking a bag of salt with you."

Scarlett ignored Des and strode back towards the house.

"What are you, girl?" Mrs Rose dropped onto one of the cane chairs with a grunt.

"I'll see what I can do to dispel any demons left behind by your brother's meddling."

"You can do that?"

Scarlett nodded.

"Then maybe it was a good thing you came instead of just him." Mrs Rose nodded towards Des.

"Maybe." Scarlett didn't bother explaining Des wasn't the one who was supposed to be here. Alex should have come and he was just as capable as she was at dealing with demons.

Scarlett walked around the side of the house. She

stopped when she saw the timber shed. It made her demon mark feel warm and her skin crawl. She straightened her shoulders and marched forward. When she stood in front of the shed, she drew her sword. Whatever demon was in there was far more powerful than Des. He only made her mark feel like a mild itch that wasn't worth scratching.

Des stood a couple of metres away from her, arms crossed on his chest and a smile of amusement on his face. "Are you going to send me to hell once you've dealt with the demon here?"

Scarlett looked over at him. "Do you feel one here too?"

"I'll exchange the information with you."

"Do you think you can talk just once without complicating things?"

He shrugged. "Probably not."

"How can you sit in my car? It's been blessed by a priest."

"Are you worried you might not be able to send me home?"

"I didn't say that. Oh, forget it. I can't believe I'm still talking to you. It's just so wrong." Scarlett turned back to the shed.

"It isn't easy. My skin feels like it's being attacked by a thousand biting insects. It also feels like the occasional knife is thrown at me too, but I think that's when you start praying in your head. I can ignore the pain." Des paused. "It's nothing compared to what a major demon can do to punish you."

"I don't kill." Scarlett continued to look at the shed rather than the demon near her.

"It isn't killing. It's more like unmaking. Now you must answer a question."

"I never agreed to that!"

"I offered an exchange of information, you asked a question."

Scarlett sighed heavily, closing her eyes. She knew talking to demons only brought trouble. Even minor ones. She opened her eyes to glare at him. "Get it over and done with."

Des smiled, his head slightly on the side as his gaze roamed her figure. "I think I'll save it. I never did put a time limit on it." His smile widened and his voice lowered. "Anticipation."

Scarlett rounded on him, opened her mouth to speak and then closed it with an audible sound. She glared at him for a moment, eyes narrowed, before she deliberately turned away and took another step closer to the shed. "Demon! This is not your home. Come out and face me."

The wind picked up. Des chuckled. Scarlett continued to ignore him.

"Demon! Show yourself. Stand before me."

"Try spilling a little blood. He'll be out in a flash. He's so very hungry. Mainly for power. He doesn't have much of his own."

Scarlett turned to glare at Des who had moved closer to her. "Do you mind?" She didn't even bother trying to keep the annoyance from her tone.

Des grinned. "Not at all." He turned towards the shed. "You might as well come out brother. She isn't going anywhere and it will only cause you unnecessary pain to resist. She will send you straight home. No punishment."

"Do you promise this, brother?" The deep voice came from the shadowy doorway of the shed.

"Brother–"

"You can't speak for me." Scarlett interrupted him.

"Give him a break, Scarlett. He's only Deception. The masks we wear when we face the rest of the world. Prayers only. No touching him with holy relics. What does it matter? He'll still be sent home."

"He can't be so minor a demon. I feel something stronger than that."

"It was the method used to call him," Des said.

Scarlett's lips thinned and her hands tightened on

her sword. That could only mean human sacrifice. "I'll give him ten minutes. Then I use holy water and my sword."

Des turned back to the shed. "You heard, brother. I have gained you ten minutes. Let her help you find the way home. No punishment if you can make it in time."

"I thank you, brother. I owe you for this favour." Deception walked out of the shed. He was half the size of Scarlett, his wiry body covered in greyish skin that seemed to ripple as he moved. His face was fluid and changed his appearance by small amounts every second.

Scarlett began to pray the moment the demon was in front of her. She noticed Des move away when she started and found that action comforting. She had worried it would be difficult to send Des home. Closing her eyes, she pushed everything from her mind but the need to send the demon back to hell. When she reached the end of her prayer, she felt her demon mark cool considerably. She opened her eyes to find she was alone. Only the power from the sacrifice, that had called the demon, causing the warmth she felt from her demon mark.

Des was nowhere to be seen. Regret crept over her and stunned by the feeling, she pushed it away, moving forward to examine the shed. Des stepped out of the gaping doorway and Scarlett smothered the shriek that came to her lips, glaring at him as she sheathed her sword.

"Tell the old woman to burn the place. There's no need to go in there."

"I'll decide that, not you." Scarlett stood in front of Des and waited for him to move.

Des shrugged and stepped back into the shed. Scarlett forced herself to move forward, fighting the urge to flee as fast as possible. Her skin crawled and her demon mark felt like it writhed beneath her skin. She glanced around the dim interior, her gaze drawn to the far end of the shed. Walking shakily forward, Des at her side, Scarlett couldn't look elsewhere.

"Why put yourself through this? You know what you're going to find. Actually, that was a rhetorical question. Answering it doesn't count."

"Stay out of my business, demon." Scarlett stopped and stared at the dirt floor. It looked like an animal had clawed and scratched at the ground, disturbed before it could make more than a shallow indent.

"Burn the shed and be done with it." His words were soft as he moved closer to her.

Scarlett shook her head. "Whoever it was deserves a proper Christian burial."

"Even if they were a murdering rapist?"

"Were they?" She opened her mouth to withdraw her question, but she was too late.

"No." Des grinned at her. "You owe me two answers."

"Then one answer will only be yes or no since that's all I gained from you."

"It was a young woman who was hitchhiking that he picked up about eighty kilometres from here nearly three years ago."

"I didn't ask for the extra information. It doesn't count."

Des laughed. "Fine. But you had best watch what you say because I'm listening very carefully. Not to mention I've already been generous. I haven't counted your 'do you mind' question."

"That wasn't a proper question." Scarlett pulled out one of the vials of holy water and sprinkled it across the disturbed grave before she hurried from the shed.

"Technically it was still a question. But I'm willing to be generous."

Scarlett took a deep breath of the untainted air outside the shed. She started to argue the point with Des, but stopped. He didn't need any encouragement. She strode to the front of the house and Des walked beside her. "Ar-" Scarlett broke off before she could finish the word. How did you ask a demon if they planned to be your shadow without actually asking a question? The best solution was to send him home, but she didn't think he'd stick around for that. Besides, it was against what she stood for. Scarlett growled in frustration.

Des chuckled.

Mrs Rose came to her feet when she saw them. "Well?"

"The demon's gone. I've got a business card in the car for a detective you need to call. Tell him you're from Father Joe's church and you're at your deceased brother's home. Say that someone mentioned your brother was interested in demons and human sacrifice and it looks like some animal has been digging up the dirt floor of his shed. You thought you'd call him first before you disturbed the area."

"Oh!" The woman staggered back to her chair. "Oh."

"I'm sorry," Scarlett said. She hated telling people bad news. They always took it harder from her. Even Alex could break bad news better. At eighteen, he was nearly a full year younger, but much better at dealing with people. "I won't be able to take these boxes for you, the police might need them. But I'll ask Father Joe to see to the taint on them and in the shed."

Scarlett retreated to her car for the business card. She strode back to the house, her gaze drawn to Des where he leaned against a verandah post. She forced herself to ignore him and gave the business card to Mrs Rose. "Do you have any idea of when you might ring? I need to call Detective Tuck after you have, to give him some other information."

The woman looked at her blankly.

"You've such a nice way about you, Scarlett." Des moved to sit beside the woman. He reached out and took hold of her hand. "I guess your daughter's going to have to listen to you say, 'I told you so'. I'm sure she hates it when you're always right."

Mrs Rose smiled shakily. "I would have preferred if she was the one saying it this time."

Des patted her hand. "You'll manage though." He smiled slowly and leaned forward. "But I'd book an appointment at your hairdresser and splurge on a new dress before those reporters come calling. You'll want to look your best when your photo appears in the newspaper." He winked at her.

"Oh, my, yes."

"I'd ring straight after you call the detective to make sure they can fit you in. You can bet the reporters will be out here as soon as they hear about the shed."

"Yes, yes, of course." She rose to her feet. "Thank you, young man. You're absolutely right of course. I'll make those calls straight away."

Scarlett turned away and strode to her car. Sitting in the driver's seat, she tucked her sword in beside her, leaning the hilt against the seat before she grasped the steering wheel. Glancing back, she saw Des putting an arm around the woman before he moved away from her. She was torn. She'd brought this demon here. Anger coursed through her. He'd been able to comfort the woman when she hadn't known the words to use. She wondered if he'd used his demonic powers, but he was such a minor demon she couldn't be one hundred percent certain. And unless she was, she couldn't intervene. She'd walked away before she did or said something she shouldn't.

She started the car as Des opened the door and climbed in. She wanted to drive off and leave him there, but it would've been wrong to leave a demon behind after getting rid of one from the property. She ignored Des who stared at her.

"I'm surprised you didn't leave me behind," Des said after several minutes. When he received only silence, he spoke again. "But I'm not going to let it go to my head. I'm sure it's only because you know you're stuck with me until you answer my questions."

"I'm wh-" Scarlett broke off before she formed another question. "You've got to be kidding me. I'm not stuck with you until I answer your questions."

Des chuckled, but didn't volunteer any information.

Chapter Three

Scarlett sat in frustrated silence. There was no way she was going to owe him three questions. She forced herself to ignore him as she drove towards home. When she saw a public phone box on the side of the road she glanced at the time on the dash. It had been about twenty minutes since she'd left Mrs Rose's house. That should have been enough time for her to have made her phone call. Parking beside the phone box, Scarlett hopped out of the car, continuing to ignore Des.

She dialled the number on a card identical to the one she'd given Mrs Rose and listened to the phone ringing. Her toe tapped as she waited for the detective to answer.

"Tuck."

"Hi Detective. Hunter here."

Tuck laughed. "Hello Hunter. Been a while since you were a woman."

Scarlett smiled. When any of her family, male or female, rang him with information they always used their surname. They'd been contacting him for years and he'd taken them seriously right from the start. "I'm wondering if you've had a call in the last twenty minutes."

"About a man who possibly summoned demons with human sacrifice?"

"That sounds like it." Scarlett gave him the address. She faced the opposite direction as Des came to stand near her.

"Yes. You have more information for me?"

"I'm afraid so. I don't know how much it'll help though."

"Fire away."

"A young woman hitchhiking. She was picked up about eighty kilometres from his place but it was nearly three years ago."

"Guess it was too much to hope for a name. Don't suppose you can help with a direction either?"

Scarlett started to turn away from Des again. Instead she looked at him thoughtfully. "Give me a second."

"All right."

Scarlett pressed the phone against her leg and continued to stare at Des. "You know if you felt like sharing any more information about the woman who was sacrificed, now would be a really good time to say it."

"Nice try. Very well worded and everything. I am left wondering what sort of information you were asking for."

"I'm not asking for any information. But if you wanted to volunteer say her name, or where she was picked up from, I'd listen."

"Now if it was a question, I could give you both those pieces of information without a problem."

"Both her first and last name."

"I could even give you her middle name," Des said.

Scarlett frowned. Demons were bad news. The woman was already dead. Making another deal with a demon wouldn't change things. Scarlett started to shake her head.

"She was seventeen and the only child of a woman who lost her husband five years ago."

Scarlett's hand curled into a fist and she closed her eyes to shut out the triumphant grin on Des' face. How could she leave that woman wondering what had happened? She took a deep breath and opened her eyes. "One question. The answer is to include the full name of the girl and where she was picked up. Exact location. And I owe you one question in exchange for it."

"Deal. Annabel May Passey." Instead of an address, Des gave her longitude and latitude.

Scarlett put the phone back to her ear. "You still there?"

"Yeah. Was beginning to wonder if you were though."

"Sorry, but I do have the name and location." Scarlett repeated the information Des had given her. "As far as I know the information is true, but the source isn't completely reliable."

"I could do with a source like that. Don't suppose you have one interested in hanging out with me?"

Scarlett smiled ruefully. He regularly asked her family that. After everything he'd learned over the years he should be more cautious about demons. "More trouble than they're worth. Trust me on that one. And I believe the young woman was seventeen at the time of her death."

"Anything else?"

"Sorry. No."

"Okay, thanks."

Scarlett hung up and strode back to her car. She drove off the moment Des was in the passenger seat.

She tried to ignore the sense of disaster she'd felt since she had unwittingly made the deal with him. It had been drummed into her from birth never to have dealings with demons. They were slippery and twisted everything. Doom! That's what he had said he'd be for her. She played the earlier conversation over again in her mind and could find no loopholes. But she wasn't a demon. How much worse had she made it by extending the original deal she'd accidentally made? She couldn't have done otherwise. How could she have left a mother wondering what had happened to her daughter? A mother who had also lost her husband.

Checking her phone, she noticed it now had coverage. Pulling over, she rang Father Joe to tell him about the demon she'd returned to hell and the young woman buried in the shed.

"Do you have something on your mind, Scarlett?" Father Joe asked when she'd finished.

"Far too much, Uncle Joe."

He chuckled. "Well, when you've finished being evasive and beating yourself up over something that probably wasn't as bad as you thought, you know where to find me."

"Thank you." She was sure he'd be saying different if he knew.

"Can you tell Gran I'll be there Saturday night for dinner?"

"Ahh, maybe you better tell her. I hadn't planned to go straight home." She wasn't about to take a demon there. That just didn't seem right. She'd go home after she got rid of him. Surely it couldn't be that difficult. She was a hunter, getting rid of demons was her speciality.

"It can't be that bad, Scarlett."

"I've got a few more things to think over first. Can you tell her I'll be late?"

Father Joe sighed. "Family doesn't judge you as harshly as you judge yourself."

"Please? I'm sorry I'm being difficult-"

"No. You go and find somewhere to think through your problems. I'll let Gran know. But, Scarlett, it was only Wednesday night that you were here for confession. I can't believe you could've got into that much trouble in a couple of days. Wait up," he said when she started to interrupt. "But if for some reason you have, there's no need for you to deal with it alone. All your family are here for you."

"Thanks."

"Go with God, Scarlett."

"You too, Uncle Joe."

Scarlett hung up and sat with her eyes closed. She

quickly opened her eyes when she felt Des' hand on hers. She pushed him away.

"I haven't come to bring you trouble. I've asked such a small favour from you. I would have offered something in exchange, but I know you would have been wary of that."

"Go away, Demon." There was no heat in her words, only weariness.

"After you have answered my three questions."

Scarlett hit the steering wheel with her palms. "You're really annoying. And stop grinning at me like that. I'm not about to become a mindless puddle at your feet and ask more stupid questions." She growled and dropped her head to the steering wheel.

"It's hard when you can't use questions. But remember, I have the same problem. I can't ask questions of you without using up the three I have left."

Scarlett turned her head to look at him, still leaning on the steering wheel. "All I have to do is get you to ask your three questions and then you're gone."

"I'll swap all questions you owe me if you will unmake me."

"I can't kill you."

"I'm not asking you to kill me. Unmake me. It's different."

Scarlett leaned back in her seat. She held up her left hand and turned her head away. "I can't talk to you. Will-" She squeezed her eyes shut for a moment. "Cancel that last word. I need you to leave me be for a bit." She turned to face him when he took her hand in his. "Let me go," she said through clenched teeth.

He raised her hand to his lips and held it there. As he pulled back, he smiled and let her go. "I will give you an hour. Maybe then you might recall how peaceful life was without me and be willing to grant my favour."

The air shimmered and Des was gone as suddenly as he'd appeared. Scarlett reached out to where he'd sat. Her hand encountered nothing. She drew her hand back to run it through her hair.

"What am I going to do now?" Her words were a whisper in the otherwise silent car. She looked at the time. One hour. That meant he'd return around dark. She had to think of where she could go before then. She considered going to her church, but she wasn't ready to see Father Joe. That left one other sanctuary, but she had another phone call she should make first.

"Hey, Scarlett."

"Allie?

"Yep."

"I-" Scarlett frowned.

Alyssa laughed. "This is Blake's phone. He's dropping me home. Did you want him to ring you back in a couple of minutes?"

Scarlett fell silent as she tried to figure out what to do. Maybe it would be best not to mention Retribution while he was driving.

"Scarlett? You still there?"

"Yes."

"Blake wants to know what's wrong."

"Maybe it'd be best if he rings me back-"

Blake interrupted her. "Scarlett."

"Blake." Her mind came up blank.

"Come on, Scarlett. We're parked out the front of Allie's parents' place. If we sit here too long, we'll have her parents out here checking on us."

"Maybe.... it might be... Allie..." How could she even mention Retribution around Alyssa after all that had happened to her? She had expected to find Blake alone.

"Where are you, Scarlett?"

This probably wasn't something that should be explained over the phone, but should she tell Alyssa too? "Can you meet me at the cemetery near your place?"

"When?"

"I'm about twenty minutes away."

There were a few seconds of silence before Blake replied. "Okay."

She finally reached a decision. "Do you think Allie can come too?"

"I don't think her parents will agree. She's still partially grounded."

"Tell them it's a prayer meeting to pray for the soul of a parishioner who's going through a difficult time."

"Who would that parishioner be, Scarlett?"

"Me."

"What about Alex and Riley?"

"Not yet. Just you two. Please?"

"Okay. I'll see you soon."

"Thanks, Blake." She ended the call and stared at her phone.

Blake was Riley's older brother and they were her only first cousins. She had plenty of second and third cousins, as well as aunts and uncles. Out of all her relatives, she was closest to Blake, Riley and her brother Alex. They had done most of their training, to be demon hunters, together. Blake was the oldest of the four of them at twenty-two and Riley was twenty, only a year older than her. Alyssa, Blake's girlfriend, was eighteen like her brother Alex.

She started her car and drove to the old cemetery. It was within walking distance of Blake's house that he shared with a couple of university students. He'd spent eighteen months away from the family and had only returned late last year. He had chosen not to stay at Gran's house with the three of them. He valued his privacy too much and you never knew which family members, or how many, were likely to descend on the house. Nor how long they'd stay.

Reaching the cemetery, Scarlett locked her car and wandered amongst the graves. Pausing in front of some of the older ones, she read the inscriptions. She slowly made her way to a grave that had an angel watching over it and dropped onto the grass beside it. She could see her car from this spot and her fingers randomly plucked at the grass as she waited for Blake to arrive. His four-wheel-drive pulled up next to her car moments later and both Blake and Alyssa climbed out of the vehicle. Scarlett remained seated as they drew closer.

They were both dressed in black jeans and shirts and wore a cross identical to the one Scarlett had around her neck. Alyssa had green eyes and dark hair, which fell in layered waves to just past her shoulders. A crimson streak curved through her hair starting at the crown on the left side of her head.

The first thing people noticed about Blake was the demon mark that circled from his wrist to his elbow.

It had been tattooed to look like barbed wire, but after an encounter with the demon Retribution, the ink was now as red as Alyssa's lock of hair. He had blue eyes, dark hair, tanned skin and a tendency to have his hair cut infrequently and shave irregularly to give him a slightly scruffy look.

They sat in the grass across from Scarlett and Blake's arm automatically draped around Alyssa's shoulders. Alyssa leaned in towards him with a slight smile.

"Okay. Time to spill," Blake said.

"Why did I think it'd be easier talking to just the two of you?" Scarlett ran her fingers through her hair. When she realised what she did, she quickly dropped her hands into her lap. "I had a demon appear in my car."

"Sounds like it might need to be re-blessed." Blake linked his fingers through Alyssa's.

"No. He said it was uncomfortable, but he could stand it since he is only… well, only a minor demon."

Blake grinned. "What's the sin?"

"Lust," Scarlett mumbled.

Blake burst out laughing.

"It's not funny." Scarlett glared at him.

"Blake, quit teasing her. A demon isn't anything to laugh about," Alyssa said.

"Sure, Allie Cat." Blake tried to suppress his grin, but gave up.

"He's trying to escape from Retribution."

Blake's grin evaporated. "What?"

Scarlett smiled wryly. "Thought that'd stop your laughter."

"You're serious?" When Scarlett nodded, Blake said, "You'd better tell the whole story. Every little bit."

Chapter Four

Scarlett nodded reluctantly. She glanced at the time on her phone. She had fifteen minutes before Des was back. She started with the demon appearing in her car, told about accidentally agreeing to exchange information with him, how she'd sent another minor demon back to hell and her weakness at the public phone where she'd ended up owing a third question to Des. Part way through her story, she noticed Des sitting on the bonnet of her car. After the first glance at him, she refused to look again.

"So if you had an hour's peace, then shouldn't he be back by now?" Blake asked.

Scarlett automatically looked towards her car where Des now leaned against her windscreen, his hands behind his head as he stared up at the stars that dotted the night sky.

Blake turned to see what drew Scarlett's attention. "Is that him?"

"But that's a man," Alyssa exclaimed.

Scarlett nodded. "Yeah."

"Come on then." Blake rose to his feet. "I haven't made any deals with him."

Scarlett and Alyssa rose to their feet and walked one on each side of Blake. Des continued to relax on the bonnet of the car, even when they stood near him. A look of amusement caused his lips to curve slightly.

"Wow, you weren't kidding," Alyssa said to Scarlett.

"Allie," Scarlett groaned.

Alyssa laughed. "Did you deliberately choose the face of an angel, Des? Or is that the face you're stuck with here on Earth?"

"Allie Cat." There was a warning in Blake's voice.

"I'm sorry, but well, he doesn't look anything like a demon," Alyssa said.

"Neither does Nathan," Blake said.

Alyssa's hands went to her hips. "Gee thanks, Blake. Way to ruin my night."

Scarlett could empathise with that feeling. Nathan had kidnapped Alyssa and tried to use her as a human sacrifice for Retribution. And now Retribution was after her. It didn't make sense.

"Demons are more dangerous than any human. I just want you to remember that." Blake reached out and tugged on Alyssa's crimson lock of hair before he turned to face Des. "I want to make it clear I'm not interested in making any deals, taking up any offers or anything else you might be hawking. I'm declining all of them now, no matter what you say or how you word it. There's nothing you have that I want and I have nothing I am willing to give you."

"A thorough man. Interesting." Des continued to recline on the car.

"What do you want with my cousin?" Blake demanded.

"Seems like you do want something from me. Answers," Des said.

"I'm trying to see if there's any way I can resolve this standoff."

"Are you speaking on behalf of your cousin then?"

No," Blake and Scarlett answered together.

Des laughed. "You must admit it was worth a try."

"Forget for a moment you're a demon and talk straight with us. What do you want, Des?" Blake asked.

"I've already explained to Scarlett. I wish her to make me cease to exist."

"You can't seriously expect us to believe that.

You're a demon. Why would you want to die when you can live for an eternity?" Blake asked.

"Not die. Cease to exist. There's a small chance I will exist again one day in the future. Slim, but worth the gamble." Des turned his dark eyes on Alyssa. "Would you wish Retribution on anyone?"

Alyssa shuddered. "No."

"I face an age of Retribution's tender loving care if I don't answer his call. You think all demons are the same. We're not. I don't gain pleasure from torturing other people. The kind of demon I am is focused on different pleasures. It's not that I won't be able to live with myself if I do torture Scarlett, it's that I won't be myself. And I've become accustomed to being me. I don't want to change. I'm actually quite averse to change."

"Wouldn't ceasing to exist be a really large change?" Blake asked.

"How can you change something if there is nothing there to change?"

"That sounds like a demon comment to me," Scarlett said. "I thought you were going to talk straight with us."

Des grinned. "I never agreed to anything. What you assume is your problem."

"Why do you have to play these stupid games?"

Allie asked. "How can we help you if you're going to keep doing this?"

"No demon would ever give up any of their power or put themselves at a disadvantage, weakening themselves," Des said.

"Does it have to be Scarlett who unmakes you?" Blake asked.

Des shook his head. "No. I knew asking her was a long shot. She's very much by the book. All demons say she sees things in black and white with no shades of grey. But she's the target. I thought it might make a difference."

"I-" Scarlett began.

"I keep telling you it's not murder. It would only be murder if a death was involved," Des said.

"Do you know what's involved in making you cease to exist?" Blake asked.

Des shook his head. "No. I was hoping you'd be able to figure it out. There are stories about a Hunter who once unmade a demon."

"Hunter as in-"

"Scarlett!" Blake said in warning.

Scarlett frowned. "You should be more specific when you use the word hunter since you could be talking about a relative of mine or using it in the accepted dictionary way." She shook her head.

"You're making it very difficult for me to help you, Des."

Des grinned. "I thought you hunters liked a challenge."

"Are you talking about a relative of ours?" Blake asked.

"Yes. But that's all the information I could get. I don't know the name, or even the year."

Scarlett ran her fingers through her hair and sighed heavily. "You can't imagine how many books our family have written, including diaries and handwritten manuals from centuries ago. This is an impossible task. And you haven't even said when you'll be asked to hunt me." Scarlett glared at Des when he remained quiet. "Arghh!"

"He's a bit annoying, isn't he?" Alyssa said. "Makes it easier to think of him as a demon."

Des leaned forward to sit crossed legged on the bonnet. "I can't give you a time. All I know is someone will receive a call when they're with Scarlett to say Nathan has slipped surveillance. It will occur about six hours after that event. Give or take a few minutes."

"Then we'll change things." Blake pulled out his phone. "Gran... yeah, she's with me... a little problem, well it's little for the moment... later Gran.

I need you to increase the surveillance on Nathan… major disaster if he slips it…. I don't have all the details and what I do have is unreliable." Blake turned away from Des when the demon rolled his eyes.

"What is it with you lot? You want me to swear an oath that I speak the truth?" Des muttered.

"Demon, Gran… Sure." Blake held the phone out to Des. "My grandmother would like to talk to you."

Des took the phone. "Venerable one of the Hunters, how are you this lovely summer evening?" Des laughed after he had listened for a few seconds. "About sixty years ago, are you still as lovely?" Des chuckled.

"He's flirting with Gran," Scarlett said in shock.

"What can you expect? That does go hand in hand with his sin," Blake said.

"Yeah, but Gran!"

"Shh! Listen," Blake said.

"I would be delighted to visit with you again, my lady," Des said.

"No!" Scarlett shook her head. "I'm not taking him home."

Blake took his phone when Des handed it to him and listened for a few seconds. "I hope you know what you're doing Gran… I'll see you shortly."

"Blake-" Scarlett began.

"Gran has spoken." Blake slid his phone in his pocket.

"But a demon?" Scarlett glanced towards Des. "And I wasn't talking to you, that was addressed to Blake so don't even think about answering it."

Blake rested his hands on Scarlett's shoulders. "Shh. Gran wants to speak with him. He's not being invited into our home. I doubt he'd be able to enter. Do you want to drop your car at my house and I'll drive you to Gran's or are you up to driving?"

Scarlett took a deep, shuddering breath. How had everything gone so wrong so quickly? "I'll drive."

"Good. And just remember, we're meant to pray for your soul sometime tonight so Allie doesn't have to lie to her parents," Blake said.

Scarlett glanced towards Des and smiled before she turned back to Blake. "How about now?"

Blake laughed. "Very mean, Scarlett. Okay, why not? I'm sure he knows better than to stick around."

Des vanished the moment they began to pray and didn't appear again until Scarlett was in her car and nearly at her Gran's house. Other than a quick glance in his direction, she ignored him.

Scarlett pulled up in front of closed double garage doors and Blake parked beside her. She looked at the spacious house caught in her headlights, the timber painted in neutral creams and browns. The gardens were lit with strategically placed lights to highlight the mass of flowering plants and shrubs. She turned off the headlights and sat in the darkness of her car.

She wanted to ask Des to leave her family alone and not to trick them or harm them. But she was having trouble thinking of a way to word such a request without it being a demand or a question.

"I know you're a demon, but I want you to remember that you're here because we're trying to help you. I would appreciate… it would… argh. Just treat my family decent," she ended in frustration.

Des laughed. "I really should be offended by that comment. But I'm too amused by the effort it took for you to get nowhere with your non-question."

Scarlett threw her door open, grabbed her sword and slammed the door shut behind her. She walked around her car to join Blake and Alyssa near the front door. Blake rested his hand on her shoulder momentarily.

"I'm fine." Scarlett sighed heavily. "Well, I will be."

The front door opened and Alex stepped out. "Gran's waiting for you around the back in the gazebo." He glanced towards the demon. "She wants you to bring him around too."

Scarlett saw the anger in her brother's dark brown

eyes, the same eyes she saw every time she looked in a mirror. His hair, the same shade as his eyes, was cut short, almost shaved. He had a square jaw, sharp cheekbones and a solemn look. At six foot, and broad shouldered, he stood out in any crowd. And unlike his cousin, most people never noticed the thin lines that snaked around his wrist three times.

Scarlett reached out with her left hand and clasped Alex's forearm so her wrist was against his. "She's never steered us wrong yet."

Alex nodded before he led the way around the side of the house, following a well-lit path. The gazebo was draped in a flowering, scented vine, the smell heavy on the warm air. There were two people waiting in the gazebo. Gran and Riley.

Riley rose to his feet and came forward to meet them. His usual smile was missing as he reached out to clasp left hands with Scarlett. He glanced towards Des, no word of greeting for him. He had sandy blond hair, short at the back and sides with a little more length at the front, warm brown eyes and a silver stud in the shape of a cross in one ear. Light caught the cross at his neck.

Scarlett walked over to her grandmother and stood in front of her, Des on her left, her family behind her. "Hello, Gran."

"There's no need to look at me like I've lost my mind, child." Gran's voice was strong, her hazel eyes ageless. She rose to her feet, the light highlighting her face, which was lined and full of hollows. Her grey hair was pulled back and plaited to just past her shoulders and her demon mark travelled nearly to her shoulder. The same thin line evenly spaced, even with the wrinkles and skin that sagged in places. She offered her cheek for Scarlett to kiss.

Scarlett dutifully kissed her grandmother. "Gran, he's a demon."

"He's asked for our help," Gran replied.

"But–"

"Enough, Scarlett. He's a creature in trouble. It's unchristian of you to turn your back on him."

At her grandmother's words, Scarlett looked at the timber floor and tried hard not to argue against them. Gran's gaze momentarily felt like a weight on her.

Gran waved to the cushioned seats built into the perimeter of the gazebo. "Sit down. No need for you all to hover."

They all sat down. Alex on Gran's left, Alyssa next to Blake near the entrance, Riley near Alex and Des reclined on Gran's right. Scarlett sat beside Des to keep a wary eye on him.

Chapter Five

"Explain to me what the problem is," Gran ordered Des. Once he'd told her all he'd said to Scarlett, Blake and Alyssa earlier, she stared at him thoughtfully as her fingers played with the cross that hung at her neck on a dainty gold chain.

"It's been a few years, Lady Hunter." Des smiled slowly at Gran. "The decades have been gentle on you."

"How old were you when you first met Des, Gran?" Scarlett asked.

"Really, Scarlett. I didn't come down in the last shower." Gran shook her head.

Blake laughed. "You'll never trick her into telling you her age."

Des leaned closer to Scarlett. "But there are other ways to find out."

She ignored his bone-melting smile and turned

back to Gran. "Have you heard of the ancestor who unmade a demon?"

Gran shook her head. "It has to have been at least a hundred years ago."

"Is that because it wasn't in your lifetime, Gran?" Scarlett tried again. The familiarity of the ritual was comfortable. She needed all the comfort she could find.

"Nor the years before I was born."

Scarlett sighed. Even the game to guess Gran's age failed to improve her humour. She glared at Des. There was only one way to do that. "Then what are we supposed to do? Read every book?"

Gran rose to her feet. "Yes. You had better get started. There are a lot of centuries to cover. I'll call in more of the family." She looked over at Des. "I'm glad to see you haven't changed either, Desire. You spoke truth back then, I pray you do today and are here to help, not harm my family."

"You have my oath I will not harm any of your family while you have Nathan under surveillance."

"Fair enough." Gran held out her hand and Des rose to take it. They stared solemnly at each other until Gran turned and walked down the path that led to the back door of the house. Des reclined on the seat again.

Alyssa checked the time on her mobile phone. "Can I take some books with me? I want to help, but I have to get home. I swear being grounded at eighteen is beyond ridiculous." When Blake was about to speak, Alyssa said, "I know, I know. I'm trying. But I think you're expecting a miracle. My parents only know one way to treat me and that's as a child. Oh well, guess you better take me back to my prison cell." She grinned. "And do you think you can spring me again tomorrow? My parents think you're a good influence on me."

Riley made a sorrowful sound. "Those poor misguided souls." He winked at Alyssa.

Alex stood. "I'll get a couple of reproductions you can take with you."

"Thanks." Alyssa rose to her feet, tugged Blake up and followed Alex.

Des continued to recline on the seat. "Almost alone again."

"Dream on." Scarlett leapt to her feet and hurried out of the gazebo. But not quickly enough that she could miss hearing Des' reply.

"Would you like me to tell you some of my dreams?"

Riley followed Scarlett into the house. "You're the last person I'd have thought to be tangled with a demon. If someone had asked me who I thought most likely, I'd have told them me."

Scarlett leaned her sword against the wall near the back door. "I'm so glad I can make you feel better about yourself."

"This might even eclipse anything Gran might hear at church on Sunday," Riley said.

"What have you done? Actually, come to think of it, what are you doing home? Aren't you meant to be at a movie with… oh, whatever her name is?"

"Whatever her name would get along fine with your demon," Riley said.

"He's not my demon."

"Yes well, he's still welcome to Sharon. That demure look and sweet personality we see every Sunday at church hides a temptress."

"Oh no. What happened?"

"Well, I don't know if I should say thankfully her parents came home or curse that they came home and are now going to tell Gran all about my corrupting influence on their daughter at church on Sunday."

Scarlett reached out and took Riley's hand in both of hers. "Tell her now, Riley. Arm her with the truth so she can deal with them. Gran will stand by you."

Riley sighed. "Yeah, I know. It's just that look she gives you when you know you've disappointed her that bothers me. It makes me feel like I'm ten-years-old."

"Tell me about it. I've still got it to look forward to when she gets me alone."

"Maybe we should stick together like glue until someone else disappoints her so we don't get to see it." Riley grinned.

"You want me there when you explain to Gran what you and Sharon were doing when her parents arrived home?"

Riley laughed. "Good point. Guess I should get it over and done with."

"And I suppose I better start reading." Scarlett sighed heavily. "Do you think it's safe to leave him out there?"

Riley shrugged. "Safe for who?"

"I don't know. Maybe I should read in the gazebo. Keep an eye on him so he doesn't disturb the neighbours or something."

Riley shrugged again. "We're never taught about helping demons and letting them hang around like guests. Only how to send them home. Your guess is as good as mine on what to do with him."

"Then I probably should read out there. I suppose he is my responsibility."

* * *

Scarlett brushed away the critter that wandered across her cheek. She tried to open her eyes, but it was too much effort. She rolled onto her side. There it was again, on her shoulder. She waved her hand near her shoulder but it was already gone. She turned onto her back again, trying to get comfortable. Now it grazed her lips. Scarlett froze, a sudden indrawn breath. Her eyes flew open to see Des centimetres from her face. His lips curved into an inviting smile.

She pressed against his chest and sat up as he moved back. "What do you think you're doing?"

"Waking Sleeping Beauty."

"Don't you ever do that again." Scarlett stressed each word.

"Even when you've tempted me for the last four hours as you muttered in your sleep. Must have been some very interesting dreams."

"Four hours!" Scarlett looked around for the book she'd been reading. She spotted it on the floor beside her with a dry leaf marking her page. "Why didn't you wake me earlier?"

Des reclined on the gazebo seat. "I was bored."

"Meaning?"

Des grinned. "Did you enjoy your dreams?"

Scarlett felt her cheeks heat. She couldn't recall the last time she'd blushed and didn't like the sensation. "You came to me for help. Stay out of my mind."

"You keep it too well guarded when you're awake. I was curious about the sleeping state." Des chuckled. "And Scarlett, you now owe me six answers, but that will change the moment you respond to my last question."

"I-" Scarlett's words became an unintelligible growl and her hands clenched as she resisted the impulse to throw the book at him. Leaving it on the floor, and out of temptation's way, she clenched her teeth. "You will have to repeat the question."

Des sat up so he was closer. "Did you enjoy your dreams?"

Scarlett opened her mouth, then shut it again. She momentarily closed her eyes and rejected each thought that came to mind. They were all questions. "Rules for answering questions weren't set."

"You don't get to pick and choose the questions you answer. I ask, you answer." Des moved even closer, his dark eyes on hers. "Truthfully."

Scarlett tried to think how to answer the question truthfully. It wasn't something that could be responded to with a yes or no. "Give me a period of grace. The first half an hour I'm awake in the morning doesn't count. I can't cope with these games straight away."

"The price is a kiss."

"You've already stolen one."

"That wasn't a kiss. Our lips barely met."

Scarlett closed her eyes and took a deep breath before she met Des' steady gaze. "Parts of them. Some of the dreams made me feel uncomfortable and during some of them I was appalled by my behaviour. I'm glad to know it was you sending them and not a product of my own mind."

Des moved back from her. "You disappoint me, hunter. I thought you more fearless than that."

"Don't try your mind games on me. I'm not going to listen or talk to you. I don't want to fall into any more traps." Scarlett bent and picked up her book. She opened it to where the dry leaf marked her place. She guessed Des had put it there. She looked over at him. He winked at her. She clenched her teeth together on the question she refused to ask and turned back to the book. It was unimportant who had saved the page she was up to.

A couple of hours later, Scarlett closed the book she'd finished reading, stretched and looked over to Des. A feeling of panic rushed through her. She was the only one in the gazebo. Rising to her feet, she stepped onto the path. When she saw Des come around the corner of the house towards her, relief made her knees feel weak. She opened her mouth to ask where he'd been, then closed it again.

Des stopped a metre away. "You look like you missed me."

"Don't wander off. I won't have you messing with the neighbours."

"Maybe you should have some breakfast. It might help your disposition."

"At least mine can be helped." Scarlett spun on her heels and stalked to the back door. She turned before she stepped inside. "Stay in the gazebo."

In the kitchen were two of her aunts and a third cousin she hadn't seen in a while. An aunt, making bacon and eggs for breakfast, dished up a plate and handed it to Scarlett saying, "Gran wants to talk to you. She's in her room. Said for you to see her the minute you came inside."

"Thanks." Scarlett grabbed cutlery and headed for Gran's room. She tapped on the closed door and waited.

"Enter." As Scarlett swung the door open, Gran placed her pen next to her notebook. She leaned back in her chair with one arm resting on her desk when Scarlett stepped into the room.

Scarlett glanced at the perfectly made bed and wondered if Gran had managed to have any sleep. "You wanted to see me?"

"Sit down Scarlett." Gran gestured towards the armchair near her and picked up a plain gold ring off her desk. She stared at the ring as she turned it in her fingers. "Life can be rather ironic at times." She turned her stare on Scarlett. "I met Desire when I was young enough to think rules were for other people. I could face any demon and send it home. I soon learned I wasn't as clever as I thought. Desire ended up saving my life."

Scarlett finished her mouthful. "Is that what this is? We're repaying a debt?"

Gran shook her head. "He asked for nothing in return. He might be a demon, but I've always had fond memories of him. People once considered demons to be gods. Not all of them were happy to be demoted to demons. But some of them could not have cared either way. Nor do they involve themselves in all the power struggles."

"We're talking B.C. here?" Scarlett asked.

"Yes. Demons have been around longer than people."

"Des too?"

Gran smiled. "Yes, Scarlett. Your demon as well."

"He's not my demon!"

"He seems to consider himself to be."

"No, he's not. Look, I made a mistake. Even you said you've made mistakes. I just want to deal with it and get rid of him."

"And you'd consign him to the tortures of the damned?"

"No!"

"It's either that or his sins become greater and he turns to violence. I wouldn't like to see a demon who has managed to resist great temptation give in now. Not after all these centuries."

"So, a bit of fornication, adultery and lust is fine?"

"No, Scarlett. And there's no need to take that tone of voice with me. What I'm trying to say is we should be doing all in our power to make sure he isn't forced into worse sins."

"Great! Now we're going to save a demon's soul, is that it?"

"You know demons don't exactly have a soul. Close, but not quite. But that term will do. It's the closest one for the situation. And yes, Scarlett. Everyone can ask for forgiveness and repent. Even demons."

Scarlett rose to her feet, leaving her empty plate

behind. She paced as she ran her hands through her hair. "This is madness."

"Scarlett."

She paused at the serious tone of Gran's voice, looking at the ring held out to her. "What's this for?"

"Take it, child."

Scarlett reluctantly took it. She noticed a faded inscription inside it. "Latin?" When Gran nodded, she asked, "What does it say? It's too worn away to read all of it."

"When you bind another to you, you are responsible to and for them."

"Bind?" Scarlett's voice was filled with uncertainty.

"It was a wedding ring that belonged to my mother. Put it on, Scarlett."

Scarlett slid it onto her right hand. The ring was loose. "Gran, why are you giving me this?"

"Don't let him lose this battle Scarlett."

"Gran? What are you asking of me?" A note of hysteria crept into her voice.

Gran reached out her hand and took Scarlett's. "I love you, child. We'll protect you from whichever demon is sent against you."

"Gran! Tell me what you're asking me to do."

"I can't tell you to do anything, Scarlett. What you choose to do is your concern. You know what's right and wrong and you're the one who will have to live with your conscience."

"You're asking me to bind him to me."

"You know I can't ask you to sin, Scarlett."

Scarlett held up her right hand. "No, but you'll give me the means to do so."

"If someone places a gun in your hand, does that mean you must pull the trigger? We all have free will, Scarlett. Now, don't forget to take your plate with you."

Scarlett stared at Gran for nearly a full minute as she tried to control the churning mass of emotions that threatened to swamp her. "I can't believe you'd force this choice on me," she said softly.

"You're old enough to be able to cope with this. I've told you the possibilities. It's up to you to choose a path."

"I'm going to find the information on how to unmake him."

"I hope you can, Scarlett. But I should warn you we've had thirty-seven people reading non-stop throughout the night. More are due in shortly and those with copies of relevant books in their own homes have been ringing to let us know which ones they can read. Some needles blend in too well in the haystack."

"Then I guess I'll have to find a large enough magnet." Scarlett grabbed her plate and strode from the room. Her anger carried her all the way to the kitchen and then to the lounge room where most of their books were stored. She took one look at the crowd gathered there, grabbed a book and fled to the gazebo.

Chapter Six

There was no peace to be found in the gazebo either. She paused in the entrance and glared at Des. She turned away and dropped down to sit on the edge of the gazebo and let her head rest against the post next to her, placing the book on the timber floor behind her. Des sat beside her.

"Wh-" Scarlett clenched her fists. A growl in the back of her throat ended the word. "I can't talk to you. Leave me alone. All I have is questions. I'm trying to sort this problem out and I can't. I just can't."

"Twenty minute's grace. Don't waste it. And it's mutual."

Scarlett stared at Des in surprise.

Des grinned. "You're wasting it."

"You have to promise to tell me when the time's up."

Des shook his head. "And take away part of the fun? Not likely."

Scarlett pulled out her mobile phone and set the alarm to go off in seventeen minutes, just to be on the safe side. "What happens if we can't find the information on how to unmake you?"

"Then I have to answer Retribution's call when Nathan makes his sacrifice."

"What kind of sacrifice?

"Human of course. But Nathan is being smart this time. It's an assisted suicide. He's promised them they'll feel no pain, only bliss."

Scarlett stared at Des and her mouth fell open. She swallowed hard. "But that's terrible. We have to talk to them-"

"You can't save the world, Scarlett. They only have a couple of months left to live. I don't blame them not wanting to live their final days in agony."

Scarlett shook her head. "You won't convince me. It's wrong. They-"

"Lady Knight, not everyone wants you to protect them."

"I'm not-" Des pressed his fingers against her lips and she pulled away from him.

"That's the way I see you. Your Gran, she was a

great hunter in her day, well and truly lived up to the family name. But you, you're a protector."

"No, that'd be Alex. Or even Blake."

"Is there a reason you find the idea of being a knight and a protector uncomfortable?"

"There are no knights in this day and age."

Des chuckled. "You may have packed away the armour, but I noticed you've kept the sword."

Scarlett sighed. It was so easy to get off track when you talked to a demon. "What are you going to do when Retribution calls you?"

"Nothing."

"But Des–"

"I will not torture you."

"He'll torture you if you don't."

"Concern for me, Lady Knight?"

Scarlett shook her head. "I don't want your pain on my conscience."

"If I hunt you, what will happen?"

"My family will protect me."

"And what are my chances of getting past your family to you?" Des smiled wryly. "Even you can see I'm still going to end up being tortured no matter which path I take. So why go to the trouble of hunting you just to postpone the inevitable?"

"If we don't unmake you in time, I can't help you

in any other way." Scarlett twisted the ring around on her finger as she tried to get it to sit comfortably.

"I haven't asked anything else of you."

"How long will he torture you for?"

The silence stretched out. Des finally answered, his voice toneless. "At least a century."

Scarlett stood up abruptly. "I can't… you can't…" her eyes closed and she tried to swallow the lump in her throat. "You're a demon!"

Des chuckled. "I fail to see what you're trying to get at."

"How-" the alarm on her phone cut her question off.

Des rose to stand beside her. "I warned you not to waste time."

"There must be another option. You can't tell me we have only the one."

"It's the only option that will fit in with your black and white view of life and sin."

Scarlett's hands tightened into fists. "Don't you start on me about sins. When you make a commitment for life, it lasts for life. You don't discard it when it's inconvenient."

"Don't tell me about commitment. I have committed to staying a minor demon and not performing acts of violence. I have spent centuries committed to my decision and I will spend a century being tortured for staying committed to my choice."

Scarlett took a step back from Des. Even though he said he didn't perform acts of violence, his anger made the air around him crackle. "I'm sorry. It's just that… well–"

"If you mention once more I'm a demon, I might make an exception regarding my rules on violence. And stop reciting prayers in your head. I'll start to think you enjoy causing me pain."

"Sorry." Scarlett turned away. She had no idea what she should do. She felt Des' hands rest on her shoulders and didn't bother to pull away. His body temperature was warmer than hers and comforting like a fire on a cold night. "I'm lost." She tensed when she realised she'd spoken the words aloud.

"That makes two of us. But I've been lost far longer than you."

Scarlett felt the warmth of his breath against her cheek and considered pulling away again. Not only was she feeling lost, but also alone. She tried to tell herself that as long as she didn't turn to face him she could imagine he was one of her family offering comfort. She sighed heavily. She wasn't going to lie to herself. Having her family's hands rest on her shoulders, and their body so close to her she could feel their warmth, had never made her heart skip a beat. She forced herself to step away and turn to face Des.

"I don't know which path to take. I always know. Normally everything is so clear. I thought it was this time, but there are certain facts I can't get my head around." She shook her head. "No, not can't! Try impossible." She fell silent as she tried to figure out what she was meant to do next.

"You're trying to make me ask a question." Des chuckled. "One question that answers exactly what you can't get your head around, both minor and major facts and why."

"If you're wanting why, that would have to be a separate question."

Des nodded. "First part of the question stands then."

"Just last week, life was simple. Demons were the enemy. Today I'm talking to you and trying to help you. That makes me uneasy. It's like the Earth suddenly decided to travel around the sun in the opposite direction. But that's not the worst of it. If I choose the correct path, I'll be choosing the wrong one. The only other option I can find is binding you to me. And I can't. That's wrong on so many levels. It's also a sin. If we can't find the information on unmaking you and I do nothing, I'm letting you be tortured. I don't know how I can stand back and do nothing. Yet there's nothing I can ethically do. I keep having that saying of 'between a rock and a hard place' play over and over again in my mind. Tell me what other choices I have, Des."

"Nathan's death will bring an end to it."

"See. Wrong. Only wrong choices." Scarlett threw her hands up in the air and turned away. "I can't choose, and yet not choosing is a choice in itself." Scarlett tilted her head back to stare at the wispy clouds. "I'd like to give the decision to someone else, but I can't. It's my responsibility. Now I can't help wondering why you bothered coming to me with this problem when finding out how to unmake you is so impossible. I'm also wondering why you didn't know that when you knew about Retribution calling you to answer Nathan's request. I hate not being able to ask questions and having to watch every word I speak." She tilted her head forward and rubbed at her eyes. "I'm so tired." The last words were a whisper.

"I can't see the future. The information was given to me by one who can, in payment of a favour owed to me. I'm sorry, Scarlett. I didn't mean to put you through all this. I truly thought you'd be able to find the information."

"I'm sorry I can't give you what you want."

Des brushed his knuckles across her cheek. "I'm glad I got to meet you." He grinned. "I can't say you'll be worth the torture, but there are moments I'll relive." He turned away.

Scarlett stepped forward and grabbed him by his shoulder, turning him to face her. She opened her mouth to ask a question then snapped it shut.

"Let me guess." He stepped close. "You want to kiss me goodbye."

Scarlett shook her head, her gaze meeting his. "I-" She ran her hand through her hair and closed her eyes momentarily. "Add them on," she growled. "What are you doing?"

"Walking away. I can't return home from here. Your place has been blessed so many times it's impossible to travel to or from hell to here."

"You can't go."

"Yes. I'm taking the responsibility out of your hands and back into mine. If you find the information on unmaking me before Nathan disappears, you have only to call for me and I'll come. But I didn't count on this. I'm truly sorry. I didn't mean to cause you all this pain."

"Count on what?"

"Your compassion for an enemy. It surprises me. Why do you care if I'm tortured?"

"I don't know," Scarlett whispered. "All I know is it makes me ache to think of you in pain." She pressed her hand against her chest. "I guess I won't make the mistake of getting to know another demon again. I can't remain objective about the prey when they become a… I don't know what you've become. To use the word friend makes all sorts of alarms go off in my head."

"I guess that would have to make me an alarming friend."

Scarlett smiled weakly. "Don't go, Des."

Before he could answer. The back door opened and Blake stepped outside. He looked between each of them. "What's going on?"

"I'm saying goodbye. Call me if you find the information. Your cousin is safe from me no matter what happens."

"No!" Scarlett shook her head. "You're not going to be tortured. I won't allow it."

"You can't protect everyone, Lady Knight."

"Are you mad, Scarlett?" Blake demanded.

"Probably. But I can't have his torture on my conscience. There has to be some way around it."

"You know all the options. You weren't happy with any of them. I'm taking it out of your hands."

Des turned to go again but Scarlett reached out and grabbed his arm.

"Scarlett-" Blake's warning was interrupted by his phone ringing. "Let him go." He answered the phone, turning away as he did.

Scarlett felt Des grow tense under her hand. She glanced between him and Blake. "No." She shook her head. Des looked at her, silently. "Tell me no. Tell me that isn't the phone call."

"Unless Nathan dies, Retribution will send demon after demon for you. Ask me to kill him. It will end both our problems."

"No. I can never ask that of you. It's one of the commandments, Des. I can't break one of the commandments."

"You wouldn't be. I would. But I can't kill a human unless it's asked of me."

"Thou shalt not kill. There's no leeway. It's clear and concise with no way of misinterpreting it. If I asked it of you, the sin would be on me too. And I thought you didn't want to commit a major sin. That you didn't want to change."

"Maybe I shouldn't be so stubborn." Des placed his hand over Scarlett's hand that was still on his arm.

"You're not going anywhere. You're not killing anyone and you're not going to be tortured. I'll figure this out somehow." Her tone was one of no compromise.

"Well you'd better hurry up. You've only got six hours to do it in," Blake said from behind her.

Scarlett whirled to face her cousin. "They lost him?"

Blake nodded and turned to Des. "Is that six hours from when they last saw him or from when I got the phone call?"

"Six hours from the phone call give or take a few minutes."

Scarlett's hands shook as she pulled out her phone to set her alarm. Blake took it off her to key in the time. She stared at the digital numbers. Six hours wasn't very long.

Blake put an arm around her shoulders and drew her close. "Will you be fine if I go and let Gran know?"

Scarlett could only nod. When Blake had gone inside, she stared bleakly at Des. Her mind was blank.

Des smiled wistfully. "Sometimes you have to admit defeat and walk away."

"I never admit defeat. I always think there must be something more I can do."

"Not this time, Scarlett."

"Wait the six hours. Please, Des."

"It won't help matters any, only make them harder for you."

"And why should you care? Better yet, why are you willing to kill for me?"

Des stared at her. His dark eyes were a swirl of emotions that Scarlett couldn't fathom. The silence between them seemed full of words. Unspoken words that when she tried to grasp them, popped like soap bubbles.

Des reached out and lightly touched her temple. "Because I know you."

Scarlett frowned. "Because… no! You didn't." She shook her head. "Tell me you didn't wander through my mind when you were playing your games this morning."

"You have nothing to be ashamed of Scarlett."

"I don't care. I didn't invite you to help yourself to my memories and thoughts."

"Then I'll invite you to wander through mine and we'll be even."

"You have got to be kidding. I couldn't do that. You're a-" she recalled his earlier comment and cut off her words.

"Demon! Go ahead. Say it, Scarlett. I'm a demon. I'm the enemy. Don't concern yourself with how I'll be spending the next century or two." He turned abruptly and started to stride away.

Scarlett hurried after him and pushed herself in front of him, placing a hand on his chest to stop him from brushing past her. "You are a demon. And you're meant to be the enemy. You annoy me so much I want to throw things. But it doesn't matter. None of it seems to matter when I think of you being harmed. I keep telling myself it's part of your power, the ability to charm people, but it makes no difference. I can't let you be tortured. Please. There must be some other way to deal with this."

Des captured her hand against his chest and stepped closer. "After those first minutes, I never bothered to try and charm you. I thought it would be a waste of time." His lips slowly curved into a smile. "Interesting."

"No it's not. I can't be friends with you. We're meant to be enemies. It's like expecting a mouse to sit down to a meal with a cat. In all likelihood, the mouse will become the dessert." Des laughed and she felt his laughter rumble in his chest under her hand. She tried to pull away from him but his hand tightened.

"Don't worry little mouse, if I have you for dessert, I promise you'll enjoy every minute of it."

"No!" She pulled away harder and Des let her escape.

"Who are you saying no to? You or me?"

"You. And we're not going any further with this conversation. What I do want to know, is if the one who told you about the future could help you find out which book you need from our collection."

"No."

"Then what else can we do?"

Des shook his head. "You know you've taken all the fun out of the game, don't you?"

"What?" Scarlett looked puzzled.

"All future questions are free and clear. But I'm going to keep five questions that you have to answer even if you don't want to. Truthfully and without reservation."

"I really hope you get the chance to ask them."

"So do I."

Chapter Seven

Scarlett finished skimming through the page and turned it. She checked her phone. Twenty-two minutes left. Not even a full minute had passed since she'd last checked. She tried to look at the next page but it swam before her eyes. She placed the book beside her and marked it with the dead leaf that had been used earlier. She rubbed her eyes and leaned back, stretching. If only Des had been able to help read the books, but they had all been blessed so no demon could destroy them. It also meant none could handle them either. Even Des with only his minor sins would not have been able to touch the books for more than a moment.

It was just her and Des in the gazebo again. Everyone else was giving her a wide berth. She sighed as she recalled all the people she had insulted or snapped at during the day. She winced as she thought of the many apologies she'd have to make. She wasn't good at apologies. They always stuck in her throat. Her gaze drifted to Des lying on the seat beside her. One leg was bent, one hand behind his head, the other across his chest. His eyes were closed and a lock of hair had fallen across his cheek.

She reached out and automatically brushed it out of the way. Surprised at how soft his hair was, she rubbed it between her fingers and thumb. The soft silky strands tangled around her fingers. She started to move her hand away and froze when she saw Des' eyes were half open and he was watching her. Her lips parted and her mouth went dry. She forced her body to move and drew her hand away from his hair. He grabbed it and pressed her palm against his lips.

"Des." His name came out as a whisper as she shook her head.

He smiled wistfully as he reluctantly let go of her hand. He sat up in a swift, yet graceful, move. "Do I get a kiss goodbye this time?"

She shook her head. "I'm so tired. So unbelievably tired."

"Then sleep. There's nothing more you can do."

"Don't say that. I don't want to hear it."

"What else can I say? Look at the time Scarlett and tell me what else I can say."

"Eleven minutes! No!" She jumped to her feet and frantically looked around. "There has to be… I can't…"

Des stepped in front of her and his hands grasped her shoulders as she started to turn from him. "Out of all the humans I have come across, I actually think you'll be the one I miss the most." There was a touch of surprise in his tone. Scarlett opened her mouth to argue but before she could voice anything, he covered her mouth with his.

Scarlett was surprised enough by his sudden move that she stood there for a few seconds and let him kiss her. The thought that she should pull away was overridden by one that this was the last time she might ever see him. Her answering kiss was filled with the conflicting emotions that tore at her. Her hands crept around his neck to tangle in his hair. Her eyes closed and the heat of his body warmed every inch of hers. Sanity tried to intrude, but she held it off for a few more minutes. She finally gave into it and pulled away. A single tear escaped and Des stopped it with a brush of his lips against her cheek.

"Take care, Lady Knight." Des stepped back and started to turn away.

"No. I can't let you go." She pulled at the ring with

trembling fingers. Grabbing his hand, she pressed it into his palm. "He can't have you."

"You'll never forgive yourself."

Scarlett laughed wildly. "Damned if I do, damned if I don't. Guess I just have to pick the sin I can live with the most."

"I can't let you do this."

"The road to hell is paved with good intentions. There are so many apt sayings for this situation," she said wryly.

"If I walk away it's no longer your concern."

"That's where you're wrong. If I turn my back on you and ignore your plight, I'd be as bad as Retribution. Please. Don't fight me on this."

Des looked at the ring in his hand and turned it so he could read the inscription. The letters seem to rise up for a second. "When you bind another to you, you are responsible to and for them." He met Scarlett's gaze. "There will be no turning back from this."

"I know," she spoke calmly. The decision was made, she no longer felt torn in a million directions.

"Then you better hurry. Nathan has nearly finished. I can feel the power build. With how strong the pull is I'd say he's only fifteen to twenty kilometres away."

The alarm went on Scarlett's phone and she turned

it off. Bending to one of the built-in seats, she lifted the lid and rummaged around until she drew out a sheathed hunting knife that hadn't been blessed. Her family had weapons stashed everywhere. Des held out his left palm to her. Scarlett hesitated.

"Hurry," Des urged.

Scarlett ran the blade lightly over his palm and a line of blood dotted his skin. She did the same to her left hand. She tossed the knife onto a seat and looked up at Des. He started to hand the ring to her then paused with it held above her right palm.

"Des, I'm okay with this."

Des smiled cynically. "I'm glad you are."

"What's wrong?"

"Promise me you won't let this ring fall into another's hands. You will wear it until I am no longer bound to it. Or if you think someone else might get the ring, release me first. I know you. I trust you. But there are many I could never trust."

"I promise." As soon as Scarlett spoke the words, the ring dropped into her right hand. She held it above her left palm and met Des' gaze. "Let yourself be bound to this ring for as long as I wear it or someone with my willing permission wears it." The ring dropped into her left palm and landed on the line of blood, to be quickly covered by Des' left hand. The ring heated in her palm and when Des drew his hand away from her, he took the ring and slid it onto her finger. She opened her mouth to protest which finger he slid it on. They weren't married. Once again, she found her words stopped by his kiss.

"Scarlett! What are you doing?" Riley rushed into the gazebo.

Scarlett pulled back from Des, half dazed. She was unable to form coherent words so instead she held up her left hand.

"No!" Riley grabbed her hand and stared at the ring. "You didn't."

Des placed a hand on Riley's shoulder. "Leave her be. This isn't your business."

"I'll-" Riley began angrily.

Scarlett pushed herself between the two of them, her back pressed against Des in an attempt to get him to move away. "I won't have you two fight. My decision. It's done. Now we have to wait and see who Retribution sends to Nathan since he can't send Des."

"It won't matter who he sends. I'll stand between you and danger," Des said.

"I can't believe you did this," Riley said softly. He pulled a tissue from his pocket and pressed it into her left hand to soak up the blood. It was quickly stained.

Scarlett smiled fleetingly. "Neither can I. Don't hate me for this, Riley."

"You're family. I'd still love you even if you killed someone." He grinned at her. "But do you think you can avoid that, I don't want to put that comment to the test."

Scarlett laughed weakly. She threw her arms around her cousin and hugged him. "Deal."

"I guess I better tell everyone the news." Riley stepped back when Scarlett let him go. He looked towards Des. "I know I live by the belief of 'forgive your enemies', but there are some things even I would never be able to forgive. Don't let any harm come to her." When Des answered him with a single nod, he strode away.

Scarlett turned to Des, placing a hand on his chest to steady herself. She stared at the ring. "I need to get it resized. I wouldn't want to lose it."

"No need." Des placed his hand over hers.

She felt his hand heat and the ring tighten. "What did you do?"

"The ring will now fit whoever wears it."

Closing her eyes, she bit back her protests about him using his demonic powers. Exhaustion had her swaying on her feet. "I've got to get some sleep before

I pass out where I stand." Her eyes popped open when she felt his lips brush her forehead.

"Call me if you need me. I can't enter the doors of your home." The air shimmered around Des and he disappeared.

Scarlett felt the ring on her finger flash with heat. She stared at it. The ring was such an innocent looking item. She stopped her thoughts before they went any further down that path. The decision had been made. She couldn't continue to dwell on it. Picking up the knife, she took it inside to clean.

Chapter Eight

Scarlett tossed in her bed and tried to escape the dreams that haunted her. The ring brushed against the cross at her throat and there was a spark of light, a flash of heat in her demon mark, pain and the sound of something crashing into the wall. She struggled to sit up, reaching for her bedside lamp and turning it on.

Des pushed away from the wall. "What the hell did you do?"

The fingers of her right hand brushed against her throat. She felt like she'd been burned.

Des crossed the room and knelt beside her bed to look at where her fingers touched. "Move your cross, Scarlett."

Still half asleep, Scarlett did as he ordered. She felt his warm fingers against the burning spot on her skin. It became warmer and then cooled. When he laughed, she looked at him in surprise. "What?"

"You're going to have to be more careful. Do you own leather gloves?"

Scarlett frowned. She played his words over in her mind and they still made no sense. "What?"

"You touched the ring to your cross. You had a burn blister there. I removed it for you."

Scarlett started to complain about him using his powers for her benefit then stopped when she saw his expression. She knew it would be a waste of breath. "What has any of this to do with leather gloves?"

"When you hold your sword, you'll burn your hand."

Scarlett's gaze dropped to her ring. There was another burn blister there. She looked up at Des. Any words she might have said were interrupted by a knock at her door.

"Scarlett? Are you okay? What's happening in there?"

"Come in, Alex." She pushed Des away from her, glad she was wearing a nightie rather than her usual brief cotton shorts and singlet. He chuckled as he rose to his feet and took a step away.

Scarlett climbed out of bed as Alex entered the room.

"What's he doing in here?" Alex glared at Des.

"I accidentally threw him from my ring. Touched it to my cross." She touched the cross with the fingertips of her left hand.

"Careful." Des tugged her hand away. "You're not the only one who feels it."

"Sorry," Scarlett said.

"Send him back to the ring before you wake the rest of the household." Alex sent a glare towards Des.

"Too late." Riley pushed him further into the room and stepped in after him. He quietly closed the door. "I've just headed off two aunts, an uncle and four cousins and someone I've never met before and wouldn't have a clue where they fit into things."

Scarlett dropped onto her bed with a groan. "Great! Just great."

Riley laughed. "Don't worry. I told them I'd take care of the problem."

"I'm sure they believed you," Scarlett said dryly.

"Well, one of the aunts did look at me rather sceptically. But if your demon could disappear again, it'd probably save you a tonne of visitors. Unless of course you were planning on throwing a midnight party." Riley glanced towards her alarm clock. "You're a few hours late though."

Scarlett looked at her clock. "Three! No wonder

you all came running." It was the worst possible time this could have happened. The hour in which demonic power was strongest. She held out her left hand. "Des, do you mind?"

Des placed his hand against hers and his body shimmered before he faded. Scarlett shuddered at the flickers of energy that played across her palm as he disappeared. She closed her hand to banish the feeling.

"I hope you know what you're doing, Scarlett," Alex said softly.

Scarlett's lips twisted into a smile and she shook her head as she gazed up at her brother. "Not at all Alex. I'm stumbling through this one second at a time."

"Scarlett!" Alex looked horrified. "That's something I'd expect Riley to say."

Riley clapped Alex on the back. "Thanks, old man."

"You do tend to be the impulsive one," Alex said.

"Unlike you two perfect specimens," Riley replied dryly.

"Enough. Please." Scarlett looked between the two of them, worried their conversation would turn into an argument.

Riley dropped onto the bed beside her and draped his arm around her shoulders to give her a one armed hug. "What can we do to help?"

"I worry when you stop smiling, Riley. Things have to be really bad when you do."

Riley grinned. "Cheshire Cat, at your service. Any other requests?"

Scarlett smiled at him weakly. "Yeah. I need ideas on where I'm going to live until this is sorted out."

"Here," Alex burst out.

Scarlett shook her head. "You saw what happened tonight. I can't stay while I have a demon bound to me. Our family has a right to feel safe."

"But-" Alex began.

"I've made up my mind," Scarlett interrupted him.

Alex continued his question anyway. "What about your safety?"

"This is my fault," Scarlett argued.

"No, it's not. It's Nathan's fault. If he wasn't such a psychopath he wouldn't have called up another demon," Alex said.

"Have you ever stopped to think about why he chose me?" Scarlett asked.

Riley grinned. "You got the short straw?"

"No. I was the only one who mocked him when we ruined his plans to sacrifice Allie," Scarlett said.

"Even if you had thrown a rock at him, this is still excessive behaviour. Leave the blame where it belongs, Scarlett." Alex stared at her until she reluctantly nodded.

"I still have to move," Scarlett insisted.

Riley's arm tightened around her shoulders. "Then we're coming too, sweetheart."

Scarlett rested her head on Riley's shoulder. "Thanks."

"You didn't think we'd let you go alone, without protection," Alex said.

"I hadn't thought. But I guess I'd have to say no. Although even if you couldn't come, I wouldn't be without protection. I'd have Des."

"And he's a real guardian angel." Alex's voice dripped with sarcasm.

"A fallen angel, maybe," Scarlett suggested.

Alex nodded slowly. "That'd make sense. But you still can't trust him. Fallen angels are fallen for a reason. You don't know what he's capable of."

"He offered to kill Nathan for me if I asked him to."

"What! Tell me you said no. Tell me you didn't even hesitate in saying no." Alex grabbed her by her shoulders.

Scarlett pulled away from Alex's hands and sat up straight, Riley's arm falling from her shoulders. "Of course I said no."

Alex rubbed the back of his neck and sighed.

"Sorry. I shouldn't have said that. I guess we're all tired and on edge. I thought it was back to routine demon hunts. The past month has been fairly quiet since we got rid of Retribution."

Riley yawned. "I don't know about you two, but I'm heading back to bed."

"I was going to put ice on my burn." Scarlett looked at the small blister on her left hand.

"Gran keeps an ointment in the fridge for burns. That'd be a better choice." Alex held out his hand and when Scarlett took it, he pulled her to her feet. "I much prefer when it's Riley making the stupid mistakes. Think you can leave it up to him in future?"

Scarlett smiled and threw her arms around her brother. "I'll do my best."

Riley stood, stretched and yawned. "Wake me when it's time to move. I could sleep for a week. It'd be nice if I could do it without printed words swimming around in my head though."

"Tell me about it," Alex muttered.

"I wonder which ancestor it was," Scarlett said.

Riley shrugged. "If they wrote anything about it, we'll know sooner or later. The crew that are still here are systematically searching each book to find the information. Gran's also been talking about having a catalogue made of all the information found in each book. It'd be a massive index. Probably need several books to fit it all in."

"They should put it on a computer database." Scarlett yawned.

Alex guided her towards the bedroom door. "Ointment and bed."

"Yes, Dad!"

"I would have thought grandpa was the better term," Riley teased.

"You're both hilarious," Alex muttered.

Riley and Scarlett looked at each other and grinned. "I know." They said in unison.

Chapter Nine

Sitting in her car with Des in the passenger seat, Scarlett looked at her list before typing the next address into the GPS she'd bought after nearly getting lost the other day. She looked at the list again. Only four more places left to see. There didn't seem to be many choices available. She was beginning to think she might have to widen her search for a house. Sharing with other people wasn't an option. There was no way she was going to involve strangers in her troubles.

"How many more hours will you continue this fruitless search?" Des asked.

"However long it takes. You want to go back in the ring?" She started the car, turning the temperature down lower on the air conditioner.

"No. And you're well aware I don't like to be part of the ring."

"Sorry. I didn't mean it." Scarlett sighed. "I guess I'm getting hungry and it's too hot to be getting in and out of the car."

"Ask me to bring a storm and it'll cool things down."

Startled, Scarlett stared at Des. "What?"

"Don't tell me you've forgotten I'm a demon," he said dryly. When Scarlett looked away, he lightly touched her chin to turn her head back again. "Scarlett?" When she didn't answer, he sighed. "The truth, Scarlett."

"It's only moments. I know you're a demon. It just slips my mind sometimes."

"The full truth, remember? If I'm using up one of my questions, you need to make the answer count." Scarlett started to turn away again and Des dropped his hand rather than fight her.

Her words were soft as she stared sightlessly through the windscreen. "Sometimes when we're doing something ordinary and you're being nice, I forget." She smiled wryly. "Actually, I even forget sometimes when you're not being nice. I–" she closed her eyes. Some words were harder to say than others, but he expected the truth. A deep breath and she opened her eyes, still facing forward. "I could almost believe you were a friend."

"People don't befriend demons."

Scarlett turned to face him as anger rushed through her. "Do you think I don't know that? Do you think I don't wonder about my sanity every time I'm reminded you're a demon? A demon!" She placed a finger hard on his chest. "You have got to stop acting so human. Stop being fun to be with. And no more humorous comments about the houses we're looking at. Don't make me laugh. Just… just… argh! I don't know. Just be a demon and stop confusing me."

"I'm being me, Scarlett. And I happen to be a demon. So that would mean I'm acting like a demon."

Her anger evaporated as quickly as it had come. "Then I wouldn't have a clue about anything anymore." Sitting here wasn't getting her any closer to finding somewhere to live. She checked her mirrors and glanced over her shoulder before she pulled onto the street.

"Scarlett-"

"No. I can't talk about this right now. I need space. I don't expect you to go back in the ring, but you could be quiet. I need that more than I need a storm to cool the day. And don't bother offering to do any more demon stuff for me. The answer is no."

"The heat doesn't bother me. I've been in much hotter places."

Scarlett ignored him and pressed down harder on her accelerator as the street took her up an incline. The streets were nearly deserted, but give it another ten minutes and the commuters would be starting to head home. She'd hoped to have found a house worth renting by now. The car reached the top of the incline and she touched her foot to the brake as she started to drive down the other side. Nothing happened. She pressed harder, but the car continued to pick up speed.

Her heart raced and she pressed her foot down until the pedal would go no further. Still no results. She reached for her handbrake and gently pulled it on. Nothing. There was a slight curve in the road and she quickly put her hand back on the steering wheel to guide the car around it. Her knuckles were white from the tightness of her grip.

"Scarlett?" Des sat up straight beside her and looked between her and the road.

Another corner loomed ahead of her, this one sharper than the last. Her mind ran through possibilities and she discarded each one. She glanced up the streets they passed, but there were no inclines to point the car at. Not that she was certain she'd even be able to get the car to take a ninety-degree corner at this speed.

"Scarlett! Ask me to do something. Please, Scarlett. All you have to do is say my name. I can't help you unless you say my name."

Scarlett opened her mouth, but no sound came out. Her hands gripped the steering wheel as she tried to guide the car around the next corner. "Des." It was little more than a whisper, but it was enough.

Des' hands gripped hers and it seemed like he flowed into the car. One minute he was beside her and the next he had moved forward, disappearing. The steering wheel was wrenched from her hand and the car slowed, taking itself around the corner. Within seconds, they had turned off the street into a smaller side street and the car parked itself near the curb.

Scarlett jumped out of the car and grabbed a large, white painted rock one of the residents had sitting in front of their mailbox. Staring at the rock she'd jammed behind her rear tyre, her legs went to jelly and she collapsed onto the grassy footpath. Des was beside her in seconds, wrapping his arms around her. She let him hold her as she tried to calm herself.

She started to pray and then stopped as she felt Des tense. Dropping her head onto his shoulder, she focused on her breathing instead. Still feeling a little shaky, she pulled back. "I've been driving for hours today. Why now?"

"The brakes were tampered with. Probably while we were looking at the last house."

"Demon?"

Des shook his head. "I would have sensed if a demon had touched the car. I wouldn't have let you in it. I guess it was Nathan himself."

Anger poured into her at the thought of Nathan touching her car. She wondered where he was now. Turning the energy into motion, she rose to her feet, pulling out her mobile phone.

"Yeah?"

"Blake. I'm about ten minutes from your place. I need you to pick me up. I've got car problems."

"What are you doing out this way?"

"Trying to find a house to rent."

"Where are you exactly? And you better be ready to answer some questions when I get there. Last I heard you'd bound a demon to you. Just because I'm not living at Gran's house doesn't mean you have to forget I exist."

Scarlett looked around. The street sign was missing. "I don't know where I am. I'm lost." She cringed at the panic in her voice.

"Is the demon with you?"

"Yes."

"Give him the phone. You can't be lost when you have a demon with you. Not regarding location anyway."

Scarlett handed the phone over and Des moved away before he spoke. She considered following him, but her legs started to feel wobbly again. She looked at Des and wondered if he was far enough away so she could start praying. She didn't even get through one line before he turned to face her, a look that clearly told her she was too close. She smiled slightly and shrugged. What could he expect? She wasn't about to completely stop praying. He'd either have to give her more space or put up with the pain.

Des ended the call and brought the phone back to her. "At least warn me."

"About?"

"Praying. It's not like I can disappear."

"What do you mean?"

"I can't go far enough away that I can't feel the pain."

"How far from me can you be?" She spoke clearly, the last few words slowly forced out.

"About thirty metres. But not for long."

"And you didn't think to mention this earlier?" Each word was almost separate, not part of a sentence.

It was Des' turn to shrug. "It isn't important."

"You're stuck with me, just about joined at my hip. You didn't think that important to mention?"

"I guessed you'd figure it out eventually. Or ask about it."

Scarlett's eyes narrowed. "Our Father, who art in heaven."

"Now don't be like that, Scarlett. It's worse when you pray aloud." Des took a step back from her, his whole body tense.

"Hallowed be thy name."

Des stumbled, backing up against the car. "Scarlett!"

Scarlett gasped at the sound of pain in his voice, remorse hitting her. She threw herself at him, her arms wrapping around him. "Des. I'm sorry. I'm so sorry."

"I can understand an eye for an eye." Des' arms encircled her waist and he pulled her close.

"Well I shouldn't be able to understand it. The bible says to love even my enemies, but I don't seem to be very good at that either." She relaxed against him.

"Don't worry about it. Besides, if you keep turning the other cheek like your gospel says, it's going to hurt after a while." His lips brushed her cheek and he leaned back to look at her.

Scarlett smiled briefly and she shook her head. "I just slip up sometimes."

"I'm glad you're not perfect."

"Why?"

"Because you wouldn't be half as interesting if you were."

Scarlett tore her gaze from his dark eyes and tried to ignore the feelings his words caused. His opinion shouldn't matter, but she had a terrible feeling it mattered more by the minute. She let him go and took a step back, his arms falling away from her.

"I'm sorry. I'll..." her words trailed off. She couldn't stop praying.

"Warn me, maybe?"

"Will that help?"

Des ran his knuckles across her cheek. "Lady Knight, life is sometimes full of pain. But if you're braced and ready for it, you can bear it easier."

"What about when you're in the ring?"

"No. I can still feel the pain. Just don't send me to the ring any more than you have to. Do you know what it's like when I'm the ring? And there is no other way to describe it other than I am the ring.

I'm wrapped around you, your warmth keeping me warm. Your pulse vibrating through me-"

Scarlett reached out and pressed her fingers against his mouth to stop his disquieting words. "There must be somewhere you can go, or something we can do to stop or reduce the pain." She started to move her fingers from his lips but he was quicker and held them there with his hand. Then he tilted her hand and dropped a kiss in her palm. A shiver went through her and she tried to pull away. Instead he tangled his fingers in hers and lowered her hand as he stepped close.

"Warn me. That's all you can do. I'll go the maximum distance from you. It won't lessen the effect by much, but that's all I can do." He smiled when Scarlett opened her mouth again and a frown wrinkled her forehead. "You can't send me back by prayers. Not now that I'm bound to you, but being bound to you also makes the pain from the prayers worse."

Her eyes narrowed. "How did you know what I was going to ask?"

"Because you're predictable sometimes, Lady Knight." He leaned forward so his mouth was near her ear. "If you want me to read your mind again, you're going to have to invite me in." This time he let her pull away. He grinned at her.

She turned from him. "Stop touching me all the time."

"Yet you're allowed to touch me? You started that." He moved so he was looking at her profile.

"I'm sorry. I'll try and remember not to. But I don't touch you in the same way you touch me."

"And how is it that I touch you?" Amusement curved his lips.

Scarlett looked over at him and slowly shook her head. "Forget it. I'm not answering that question."

"I could make it a question I'm seeking the truth of. I do have four of them left."

Alarm flared in Scarlett's eyes and she took a step back. She opened her mouth to disagree and then thought better of it. She didn't want to risk him thinking it was a challenge.

"How about I offer you two questions in exchange for you being able to truthfully say you hate it when I touch you. I'll leave you be if you can tell me it completely disgusts and sickens you." When Scarlett looked away, he smiled mockingly. "That's what I thought." He strode over to a brick mailbox and sat on it.

Scarlett fought the urge to go comfort him. She

tried to remember he was a demon, but it was becoming more difficult. Instead she turned her back to Des and watched for Blake. She was relieved when he arrived five minutes later. "What took you so long?" she demanded before he was barely out of his four-wheel-drive.

"Are you okay?" He rested his hands on her shoulders and stared down at her.

"Yes. Now what took you so long?"

Blake glanced over to Des who still sat on the mailbox, one leg drawn up so his chin could rest on his knee. "What's going on?"

"A difference of opinion."

Blake chuckled. "What did you expect? He's a demon."

"I'm still waiting for you to tell me what took you so long."

"I had to organise a tow truck."

"Oh! I didn't even think about that."

"I'm not surprised. You were probably feeling a little shaken. It's difficult to get my head around the fact I owe a demon for saving your life."

"What did you two discuss on the phone?" Scarlett's eyes narrowed. "You could have asked me."

"And you would have told me everything was fine

and glossed over what happened. Forget it. I asked Des instead."

"Talking of people glossing over a question, what aren't you telling me?"

"Guess we know each other too well." Blake sighed. "I had to tell Gran."

Scarlett tensed and opened her mouth to yell at him. Instead she took a calming breath and slowly let it out. "Okay, so you told Gran. What did she say?"

"That she'd have a house for you to stay in within a few days."

"Come on, Blake. You're not going to expect me to drag every little bit of info out of you, are you?"

Blake smiled. "I had considered it." He stepped to the side as she threw a light punch at him. "Okay! Truce." He glanced over to Des who had moved closer when Scarlett had battled her anger. He turned back to Scarlett. "She's going to buy a house. Said it's probably past time the four of us had a place of our own, but if we invite Alyssa to move in, she'll evict the lot of us." Blake grinned. "The thought had crossed my mind, but I know my limitations. She's trying to find something close to the cemetery so we have sanctuary nearby, if we need it."

"I can arrange for a person, with a house backing onto the cemetery, to want to sell," Des suggested.

"No," Blake and Scarlett said together.

Des shrugged. "You people really have no idea what it means to have a demon bound to you, do you?"

"We know," Blake said softly.

"We don't approve of slavery," Scarlett said. "I'll make no demands on you. I want you to use free will."

The tow truck picked that moment to arrive and they were kept busy for a while. It wasn't long before they were in Blake's vehicle and driving to Gran's house.

"Where am I meant to stay while Gran buys a house?" Scarlett asked.

"With me. One of my housemates isn't back from spending Christmas with his family. He won't return until just before uni starts for the year. And my room is the only one protected against demons so Des should be able to cope well enough," Blake said.

"We'll stay there tonight?" Des asked from the back seat.

Scarlett half turned in her seat to look at him. "Yeah."

Chapter Ten

By the time Blake left Gran's house late that afternoon, not only did he have Des and Scarlett in the vehicle, but also Riley and Alex who had refused to be left behind. When Blake's housemate, Greg, saw the crowd, he argued with Blake about taking over the place.

Scarlett didn't know what Blake told Greg, but he grabbed a handful of clothes, jammed them in a plastic bag and stalked out with a glare for each of them.

"Does he know you're moving out soon?" Scarlett asked Blake.

Blake nodded. "Yeah. That's part of why he's not happy. He also said you're to have his room, that he's not having the other three in his room, or his bed." Blake shook his head at Scarlett's questioning look. "Let's not get into that explanation."

Scarlett strode to the bedroom in question and opened the door. "I hope you've got spare sheets. This room's a pigsty. I'm beginning to think I'd rather sleep in the lounge room."

"You can't sleep on the couch, there's so many valleys in it you'd be awake all night," Blake said.

"What about your swag?"

Blake stared at Scarlett. "You're serious, aren't you?" She nodded. "It's in my room, under the bed. I'll bring it out later."

"And what about us?" Alex asked. "You're not expecting me to share a bed with Riley, are you?"

Blake shook his head. "There's a trundle under Allan's bed for when his sister's in town."

"I've got Allan's bed." Riley grinned at Alex who shook his head and muttered something about children under his breath. "Sticks and stones, but you've still got the trundle."

"What about Des?" Scarlett asked.

"I don't need to sleep as you do. When I sleep, it's for pleasure."

Scarlett frowned. "How can sleeping be for pleasure?"

"Sometimes I think you're a hopeless cause."

"If by hopeless cause you mean you can't corrupt me, then yes, I am one," Scarlett said.

"What are you going to do while we're asleep?" Blake asked Des.

"Watch over all of you."

"Watch-" Alex broke off his words at the look his sister sent him. Instead he stalked to the bedroom that was to be his and quietly closed the door.

Riley laughed. A short, sharp sound. "What do you think you are? A fallen guardian angel?"

"None of us are perfect, Jester."

"How sweet. I get a nickname too," Riley said dryly. "I should probably be offended that I'm not Sir Jester." He glanced over to Scarlett. "After all, Scarlett and Gran have the title of Lady."

"Titles have responsibilities attached to them," Des said.

"Enough." Scarlett stepped between the two. "I don't like where this conversation's going."

Des nodded and moved over to the couch, sitting on its arm. Riley looked like he'd speak, but when Scarlett continued to glare at him, he shrugged and smiled.

"Guess I better make sure Alex doesn't steal the bed."

Scarlett watched as Riley walked away from her. She sighed then looked over to Blake who watched her carefully. She raised a brow but he shook his head in answer.

"If we're already arguing, what will we be like a week from now? Or even in a year if we can't solve this issue." Scarlett waited for Blake to answer.

"If we're lucky a bolt of lightning will strike Nathan dead and we won't have to worry about that," Blake said dryly.

"Do you-" Des began.

"No." Blake and Scarlett answered together as they turned to look at him.

Des smiled mockingly. "I have to check. One day you might change your mind."

"Never," Scarlett said fervently.

Des turned his gaze on Blake, the smile still evident. "No more protests from you?"

"A man never truly knows how he'll react when all hope is lost and his loved ones are in mortal danger." Blake met the dark eyes squarely.

Des nodded and turned to Scarlett. "Give me permission to follow orders given by Blake."

"No!" The word burst out automatically.

"The offer of free will didn't last for long," Des said. His tone indicated he hadn't believed the offer anyway.

Scarlett moved over to him and took his hand. "I

can't give you that permission on the heels of what Blake said. But I do give you permission to follow or dismiss any orders given to you by anyone and to follow your own plans and thoughts."

Des rose and leaned forward so his mouth was near her ear. "All my thoughts?"

Scarlett pulled back and tugged on her hand. Des held tight. She glanced over to Blake who continued to watch her carefully, his arms crossed over his chest.

Scarlett took a deep breath and slowly released it. "You're not to infringe on the free will of others in following your plans and thoughts." She tugged on her hand again and he let it go.

"A pity."

Scarlett breathed deep again. She couldn't find her usual calm. "You asked me to warn you when I plan to pray."

Des nodded. "I'll wait outside."

As soon as Des left the room, Blake walked over to Scarlett. "He's not human."

"I know."

"Always?"

Scarlett sighed. "Even when I forget, I still know. It's not that type of forgetting. It's more that my mind can't connect Des to what I know about demons so it temporarily rejects the idea he's one."

"Maybe it'd be best to hand the ring over to me and take yourself away from him."

"No." Scarlett looked away from Blake's uncomfortable gaze and wished she hadn't answered so quickly. "No. I couldn't."

"Why?"

"What do you want me to say? That he's my responsibility and therefore I should be the one to keep the ring?"

"I want you to say what's true."

Scarlett laughed sharply. "When I figure it out I'll tell you."

"Scarlett–"

"I know. You don't have to tell me. I owe so many apologies to Allie."

"What?"

"I was horrid to her when we first met. How could I have been so unbending? As far as I was concerned we were wasting our time on a sinner who'd go straight back out and make more stupid choices. My path has crumbled under my feet leaving a little track clinging to a cliff. It has completely disintegrated in places leaving me no choice but to leap and hope I can jump far enough. I never realised how disorientating that was. I always knew exactly where I was headed. And which choice to make since right and wrong are so clearly defined." Scarlett laughed again. The sound was brittle. "If pride goeth before destruction, and an haughty spirit before a fall, then I guess I'm in for a big one."

"We'll be there to help cushion your landing."

"Thanks. You mind if I have some time alone? I need to pray. Maybe then I'll find some of the peace that's eluded me lately."

"Call me if you need anything." Blake dropped a kiss on her forehead before he left the lounge room.

* * *

Scarlett sat up, her heart racing when the lounge room light being flicked on jarred her from sleep. She squinted at the brightness and opened her mouth to complain to Des who stood by the switch, wearing only jeans. He nodded towards the lounge room window off to her left and she turned to look. She scrambled to her feet, grabbing her sword, her gaze fixed on the demon coming in the window.

There was a flash of light and she shrieked, dropping her sword. Cradling her left hand she turned to see Des grab the door frame. Regaining his balance, Des strode to the centre of the room. There was a sound of running footsteps then Blake, Riley and Alex stopped in the doorway. Each carried their swords and none were dressed in more than shorts or boxers. Their attention was immediately drawn to the demon who warily stood in front of the window, looking at each of them.

Scarlett bent to pull a soft, black leather glove onto her left hand before she picked up her sword again, waiting to see who the demon would attack first. Blake, Riley and Alex moved to her side.

Scarlett wished she had time to pull on jeans over the brief cotton shorts she wore with a singlet. She'd worn her jeans to bed, replacing them when they'd been too uncomfortable to sleep in. Her gaze remained on the demon wondering what he was waiting for. Did he wait for them to attack first?

He was a similar height to Des, but there the similarities ended. His skin was as black and glossy as a brand new tyre. His hair, the colour of dried blood, was pulled back from his face to hang between his wings that matched his hair. His clothes looked like they were made from the same material as his skin, so closely did they match and streaks of red flames shot through his black eyes.

The demon finally launched himself at Des, who met his attack in mid air. Black wings springing from Des' back as he flew to meet him. The demon snarled.

His hands turned to claws and he swiped at Des. Scarlett watched the block and attack of the battle. They covered every centimetre of the small lounge room, knocking an armchair over in the process. Most of the fight happened in mid-air, the two demons evenly matched.

They were on the ground again and warily stalked each other as they looked for weaknesses and openings. Des kept his gaze on the demon. "Scarlett, drop your sword. Remove your glove."

"What are you doing?" Alex hissed when Scarlett lowered her sword to the floor.

"What does it look like?" Scarlett snapped.

"We don't follow the orders of demons." Alex grabbed her right hand as she tried to tug off the glove.

Scarlett met her brother's gaze and used her teeth to pull the glove from her hand, letting it drop to the ground. "He promised to be my guardian angel. I trust him to protect me."

"You're mad!"

Riley tried to put his hand on Alex's shoulder, but he shrugged it off. "We're here too. She's not unarmed as long as we're beside her."

"Scarlett! What's taking you so long?" Des demanded as the demon launched at him again.

"I'm ready," Scarlett said.

"When I say now. Hold your cross." Des' wings launched him from a standstill and he grabbed the other demon and yelled, "Now." He kept his arms locked around the demon that struggled to escape.

Scarlett closed her hand around the cross, pressing it against the ring. Heat flared in her hand. Scarlett screamed while the demon roared and disappeared in a flash of light. Des stumbled forward, his arms now empty. He landed on his knees, one hand pressed against the floor. Letting go of the cross, Scarlett staggered towards Des, dropping down in front of him to wrap him in her arms. She shivered. It felt like holding energy. She drew back enough to meet Des' gaze. They were flame-streaked.

Des laughed derisively at the shock in her eyes. "Now do you believe I'm a demon?"

She could hear movement behind her, but she ignored her family. Instead she hesitantly touched a wing, surprised at how soft the feathers were. "I've always known you were a demon," she said softly. "But for some reason that seems less important each day."

Des' voice was equally quiet but there was no softness in his tone. "If your family weren't here I'd show you exactly what sort of demon I am."

"I don't believe that."

"Then you're a fool."

"Yeah, I'm starting to think that too." Scarlett began to pull away, but Des put a single hand on her back to stop her.

He lowered his head until his cheek was against hers, his lips against her ear. "If we're ever alone and I become completely demon… run."

"No. I trust you."

Des' arm around her tensed. "You've been warned."

Des let her go and Scarlett pulled back. She noticed a feather in his hair and reached out and took it. Des grabbed her wrist. He stared at her as the flame streaks started to fade from his eyes.

"What do you want my feather for?"

"You can't leave it lying around for someone to use against you." She continued to meet Des' gaze until he let her hand go. Rising shakily to her feet, she glanced around. She noticed her family by the window, a whispered argument keeping them there. She saw the saltshaker in Blake's hand and sighed. How could she tell him salt across the entrances wasn't the right choice? She had bound a demon to herself. A little salt was harmless in comparison.

She walked back to the swag and slid into it. She

scrunched down until her head was covered, the feather still clasped in her hand. Was this how it happened? You commit a sin and suddenly lesser ones weren't so important? She couldn't accept that. She had to believe she could still manage to keep her life as unblemished as possible. Hunting demons was all she'd ever wanted to do. And you couldn't do that with a soul so stained by sin you were little better than your prey. Yet now she had a demon bound to her and she had a terrible feeling that her worries about calling him a friend were no longer an issue. No, she wanted a much deeper relationship than that. She squeezed her eyes shut and started to pray.

"Scarlett!" Des bellowed. "You said you'd warn me when you prayed."

She stopped. What else could she do? Hadn't he already endured enough pain for her tonight?

Chapter Eleven

Scarlett stretched, her eyes still closed, and started to open her hand. It felt cramped. Then she felt the movement of the feather and kept it closed. She should do something to make sure the feather couldn't be used against Des, but she had no idea what to do.

Unzipping the swag with her left hand, she pushed back the cover. It was too hot to stay under it, even though it was now only drawn up to her waist. Her eyes slowly opened and she froze. Des sat on the floor a couple of metres away from her, crossed legged, his dark eyes fastened on her.

She sat up and her gaze roamed over him. His wings were gone and his eyes were a solid darkness. "What are you doing?"

"Well, I could say I'm watching over you."

"You could?" She thought over his words. "What should you say instead?"

Des' lips slowly curved into a smile. "Flirting with temptation."

"What?"

"Another ten minutes and I would've lost."

Scarlett discarded several questions before she settled on one to ask. "What is the temptation?"

"Your dreams. I can't dream. Fantasize, yes. Dream, no. I was very tempted to share yours."

"You have a real problem with boundaries, don't you?"

Des laughed. "You could say that's what set me on this path. So what do you say? Can I share your dreams?"

"No."

"What if I promise to stay out of the rest of your head and not to alter anything unless you ask me to?"

Scarlett wavered at the look he sent. "No." The word came out softer, less commanding. She quickly rose to her feet before she gave in.

"Just once?" Des persisted.

Scarlett ignored him and wandered over to the window. She looked down at the ledge where a row of salt lay. Blake had won the argument.

"I was wondering when you'd wake up."

Scarlett spun to face Blake.

"No comments about the salt?" Blake asked when she remained quiet.

"He that is without sin among you, let him cast the first stone," Scarlett quoted.

"Ahh, Scarlett." Blake strode to her side and wrapped his arms around her. "Back off demon, I'm not going to harm her."

Scarlett pulled away enough to be able to see Des. She didn't know what his expression meant, but if she had to guess, she'd say jealousy. She discarded that thought and inwardly laughed at herself.

"Scarlett." Blake drew her attention back to him. "You can still take a stand against things like using salt across entrances."

"It seems hypocritical."

"Being irrational is part of being human. We don't always make sense."

"I guess," Scarlett said softly.

"I know." Blake's voice was filled with certainty.

"Where are Ry and Alex?"

"With Gran. She's giving them a list of houses to look at and the requirements."

"Why didn't she ask me? Or you as well, for that matter?"

"She did. But I think Riley and Alex need a break

from the situation. They're not dealing with having a demon as a guest. It goes against all we've been taught."

"Why are you managing when they're not?"

Blake left one arm around her and guided her towards the kitchen as he answered. "I guess I had to learn tolerance while I was away from our family. There isn't a lot of job opportunities for someone with a half completed degree in anthropology. I came in contact with a lot of interesting people when I was working at the nightclub. Without learning tolerance, I wouldn't have lasted."

"You could have returned home."

"No. I had to sort myself out first. Seeing someone die like that…" His voice trailed off as he shook his head.

"Did you ever do anything you regretted while you were away from the family?"

"It all depends on how you look at things."

"How do you look at them?"

"I did things it was possible to regret, but how can I regret things that helped shape who I am. My mistakes helped me learn to survive on my own two feet." Blake pushed her towards one of the chairs at the kitchen table. "Enough soul searching. It's breakfast time."

Des stood in the doorway. "And who exactly does that invite include?"

Blake gestured towards the table. "If you want to join us, have a seat."

Des sat directly across from Scarlett as Blake began to crack eggs into a bowl.

* * *

Scarlett rose to her feet and paced across the lounge room again. She slumped onto an armchair, tried to get comfortable then rose to pace across the room another couple of times before she dropped onto the couch.

"I can't stay in here. I have to get out." When Blake continued to read, she demanded, "Did you hear me?"

Blake glanced up from his book. "You're safe here and the salt doesn't bother Des unless he tries to cross it."

"I know I'm safe. Physically. If I have to sit here a minute longer, I can't vouch for my mental well being." She was accustomed to being a lot more active. Pacing through a handful of rooms wasn't enough to keep her occupied.

Blake sighed, dropped his bookmark into the book

and reluctantly closed it. "What do you want to do, Scarlett?"

Scarlett rose to her feet again. She tucked her fingers into the front pocket of her jeans and they brushed against the feather. "I don't know. I just can't sit around and wait."

"I'll guard her." Des stood by the window and watched the traffic. He turned to face Blake when he didn't answer.

"Is that what you want?" Blake asked Scarlett.

She shrugged. "I just want to get out. I don't want everyone hovering over me. Besides, I know you cancelled plans to be with Allie so you could babysit me. You should go and see her."

"Your safety comes first."

"I will be safe. Do you think Des is going to let something happen to me?"

Blake laughed cynically. "No, but not for the same reasons you do. He has literally put himself in your hands." He looked at the ring Scarlett wore on her left hand. "He has his own interests to protect."

"Blake-" Scarlett started to argue but Des interrupted her.

"He's right, Scarlett." He moved away from the window and stopped within arm's reach. "I'm a demon. We always put ourselves first."

"I don't-" Scarlett began.

"Do you want to go out or not?" Des asked.

"Yes."

"Where are you going?" Blake asked.

Scarlett shrugged again. "I don't know. Maybe we'll catch the ferry and go into the city and wander around until we find something to do."

Blake turned to Des. "Hell won't be far enough if something happens to her."

Des grinned. "I much prefer Old Testament Christians and their belief in an eye for an eye."

Blake's expression stayed serious. "Let's just say I have trouble following New Testament principles when one of mine is threatened or harmed. Instinct outweighs clear thought."

"I let instinct regularly interfere with clear thought. It keeps life much more interesting. Self-preservation is a well-developed instinct. I'll return her with her life intact. Her soul though, that's not my concern," Des said.

Blake nodded. "That's all I ask. She's responsible for her own soul."

Des turned to Scarlett. "You'll have to brush the salt away from the doorway before I can leave."

Scarlett nodded. She kissed Blake's cheek and then rubbed it. "You need a shave."

Blake chuckled. "Allie doesn't think so." His expression turned serious. "Take care, Scarlett." He glanced towards Des, a warning in his eyes.

Scarlett nodded before she strode towards the front door. She bent down and pushed the salt into a small pile against the wall. As she stood up, her hands brushed her back pockets to make sure her wallet and phone was in them. She wore no cosmetics and her hair required minimal attention. All she needed was her slim wallet and mobile phone. Sometimes she carried a backpack with emergency gear. Usually it stayed in her car. She didn't think she'd have any need of it today. After all, she had a fallen guardian angel on duty.

As they walked along the footpath in the direction of the ferry Des linked his fingers through hers. "What do you want to do?"

Scarlett shrugged. "I really don't know. But walking outside is so much better than pacing back and forth in a small room."

"Do you need help with some ideas?" His lips slowly curved into a smile and his voice lowered as he turned his head to watch her.

"No thanks," Scarlett said dryly.

Des chuckled softly. "I'm sure I could find lots of

things to do that would take your mind off your problems."

"Yeah and have me worrying about other problems. My soul might not be perfectly spotless, but that's what I aim for."

"Think how much more interesting it could be."

"More interesting than sharing a house with a demon?"

Des laughed. "Touché."

They reached the ferry shelter to find they were the only ones waiting for the ferry, which arrived on time. Scarlett started to step onboard when a wave made the ferry rock dramatically. Des reached out to steady her. She smiled her thanks and quickly boarded when the ferry's movements evened out. As soon as she payed for their tickets, she led the way to the bow. She loved seeing where she was going and feeling the breeze in her face.

Holding onto the rails, she closed her eyes to savour the sensation of movement on the water. She felt Des come to stand behind her. His hands gripped the rails on either side of her hands and trapped her in his embrace. Scarlett leaned back against him and relaxed as a feeling of safety washed over her.

"When I was younger I wanted to sail around

Australia. I had very romantic ideas of what it'd be like." Scarlett's eyes remained closed.

"Do you still want to do that?"

"Only when life's difficult."

"You have only to ask and we can go," Des said softly.

"Somehow clicking my fingers and there it is doesn't appeal to me. It feels like cheating.

Des laughed. "Remind me to play poker with you one day. I like to win."

"I'm not an idiot. You'd probably cheat."

"There's no probably about it."

Scarlett smiled and turned in his arms so she could look at him. "How about we see a movie?"

"Why do I get the feeling the movies you'd be willing to see would bore me to tears?"

Scarlett laughed. "We could always see if there's one we'd both like." Des smiled and Scarlett stopped. "Why am I starting to worry a movie isn't a good choice?"

Des leaned in closer, his voice low. "Sitting next to each other in the dark, what's not to like about that?"

Scarlett pulled out of his arms and stepped to his right. "Maybe we should find something else to do."

Des chuckled. "Coward."

"Didn't you mention something about self-preservation earlier?" Scarlett glanced over the side of the ferry as it began to slow. "Come on. We're nearly there."

As soon as they were off the ferry, they headed for the cinemas and finally found a movie they could agree on. Scarlett spent the first half of the movie trying to get Des to behave. Holding his hand had seemed like a way to keep him in line, but she ended up spending the other half of the movie alternating between wondering what she was doing holding hands with a demon and wanting to always hold his hand.

When the movie finished, they wandered outside and Scarlett pointed to an ice creamery over the road. She turned to smile at Des.

"What do you think?"

He leaned in close and murmured against her ear. "I have some very fond memories involving ice cream."

Scarlett pulled away. "Oh for crying out loud, Des. Does everything have to remind you of sex?" She glared at the two young women who walked past them and giggled.

One of them called out to Des, "Honey if she doesn't know what to do with you, I do."

Des smiled unhurriedly as he draped his arm

around Scarlett's shoulders. "She knows what to do with me." He lowered his voice so only Scarlett could hear him. "You just like to deny both of us."

Scarlett remembered to keep her voice lowered this time. "I am not stopping you from going with them."

"Funnily enough, the thought of going with them bores me. I fear you're beginning to rub off on me, Scarlett. Which doesn't bode well for my future as a demon of desire."

"Maybe it's time for a new career."

Des laughed. "You're priceless." He kissed the tip of her nose. "Now, didn't you say you wanted ice cream?" At her nod, they began to walk to the curb and waited until it was safe to cross.

Chapter Twelve

Scarlett stared at the old building across the road that had scaffolding across the front so workers could paint it. She brought her attention back to the road when Des started to move forward. He kept his arm around her as they meandered along the footpath and even though she felt she should pull away from him, Scarlett couldn't bring herself to. They reached the scaffolding when Des suddenly threw his other arm around her and propelled her forward. They landed on the ground, Des underneath her.

Scarlett looked down at him, stunned and confused. She pushed herself back and glanced around at the crowd that had begun to gather. Then she saw what they looked at. A twenty-litre tin of paint, that had been full, lay open on the footpath. The paint seemed to be everywhere, but luckily Des had pushed them far enough out of the way the splatters had missed them. Scarlett started to shake as she realised it had landed in the exact spot where they'd been when Des had wrapped her in both his arms.

Des sat up and moved Scarlett off him so he could stand. He pulled her to her feet and held her close. "You're safe," he murmured against her forehead. "I won't let anything happen to you."

Scarlett took a deep breath. "I don't like being prey. I'm a hunter." If Des hadn't been with her she would have noticed another demon before he'd got that close.

"What do you want to do?" Des asked.

Since it wasn't dark yet, Scarlett knew the demon would be a minor one. "Can we track him down?"

Des lifted his head and slowly looked around. He paused and turned his head back slightly. His lips curved into a mirthless smile. Tiny flickers of flames streaked through his eyes. "That way."

"Des," Scarlett began hesitantly, as she looked into his eyes.

"I'm fine, Lady Knight. I'm still a long way off. Can you see wings yet?" When Scarlett shook her head, he took her hand and tugged her forward. "Then let's hunt."

Scarlett strode along beside him, almost running to keep up. "I haven't anything with me."

"You have the ring and the cross. It'll do the trick."

"It hurts you."

Des chuckled. "It hurts you too."

"Yes but–"

"Lady Knight," Des teased.

Scarlett fell silent and concentrated on keeping up. She glanced at Des who was not in the least out of breath, nor did he have sweat dotting his brow and upper lip like she had. Some things were plain unfair.

Des swore and came to a sudden stop.

"Des!"

"Quiet." He turned his head as if he listened for something. His head stilled and his eyes gleamed.

Scarlett glanced around nervously. Demons she could face. But the area they had stepped into didn't look friendly in the last rays of the day. There was no one in the vicinity and it was filled with an unnatural silence. There were a couple of large industrial bins along one wall and the buildings towering over them were several storeys high, dotted with windows and balconies. Des distracted her when he pulled his shirt over his head and handed it to her.

"What are you doing, Des?"

"Quiet. And stay back until I'm in full control

again." He cupped her cheek with his hand. "For luck." Before Scarlett could ask what he meant, he swiftly kissed her and turned away. Wings sprang from his back as he launched himself into the air.

She watched as a demon seemed to leap from the brickwork and attack Des. The demon took on the colour of whatever he touched, like a chameleon. His wings were leathery with sharp hooks at the end of each segment. He had goat like horns and a habit of lowering his head to attack with them.

Scarlett hated to be a spectator. She looked around, but there was no way she could help. They flung each other from balcony to balcony, bodies impacting with walls and each other. Her left hand hovered over her cross as she waited for Des' call. But the chameleon seemed to break Des' every hold. The shadows rapidly lengthened until Scarlett had trouble seeing the fight.

Then she was only able to tell where they were by the snarls and thuds. And still her hand hovered over her cross. "Be safe, Des," she whispered. Her phone rang and she considered ignoring it. She held it in her right hand to answer it, her left still above her cross. "Yes?"

"Where are you?" Alex demanded.

"We went to see a movie."

"I was expecting you to be here when we got back. Blake said you've been gone for hours."

"You're not my father, Alex. You're my brother."

"Then maybe Dad should be home to make sure you listen and keep yourself out of danger."

"Alex I'm-"

"Now!" Des yelled.

"Call you back," she said as her hand closed around the cross. She managed to end the call before she screamed at the pain. There was a flash of light and a roar that was cut off.

"Let go, Lady Knight." Des' voice came out of the dark, tense with pain.

Scarlett let go, dropped to her knees and breathed heavily. She shakily rose to her feet and took an unsteady step forward. "Des?"

"Run!"

"Des?"

Des swore and snarled, "Now! Find people."

Scarlett spun and ran back the way they'd come. Stumbling in the dark she slowed her pace, not wanting to fall. She glanced over her shoulder, but could hear nothing. As soon as she stepped into a well-lit street, she took a deep breath. There were a handful of people wandering past. Glancing behind her again she felt torn. She didn't want to desert Des, but he hadn't sounded like himself.

Her phone rang and she checked the display to see it was Alex again. "Sorry."

"What's going on? Where are you? I'll pick you up."

"Everything's fine."

"Don't give me that rubbish. I know you. What did he do?"

"Alex-"

"If he hurt you-"

"It was another demon."

"Where are you?"

Scarlett glanced behind her again and wondered where Des was. She knew he wouldn't be too far. Thirty metres at the most he'd told her. Sighing, she looked at the street sign, giving Alex the information he wanted.

"I'll see you in about half an hour." Alex hung up abruptly.

Scarlett stared at her phone before she returned it to her pocket. Minutes passed as she stood there, wondering what to do. "Des. Where are you?" She didn't expect an answer to her whispered question and felt relief when she received one.

He stepped out of the shadows and held out his

hand for his shirt. "You don't listen very well, do you?" He pulled on his shirt.

Scarlett threw her arms around him and held him close for a minute before she leaned back to look at him. "You aren't hurt? Don't smile at me like that. I hate being patronised."

Des chuckled. "Only you would ask a demon if they were hurt. We can't be killed, Lady Knight. Surely they taught you that."

Scarlett glared at him and tried to pull away. "You can still be hurt." She turned her head when he tried to kiss her and his lips landed on her cheek instead. She felt him smile against her before his lips trailed down to her neck. "Des!"

"I thought that's what you wanted," he answered innocently.

"I don't want any kisses."

"Try saying that again, but put more conviction in it."

Scarlett sighed. "Let me go, Des." She pulled away and his arms loosened. Before she could move too far, his fingers tangled with hers.

"Nathan can't send another demon for you until three in the morning. Not with the amount of demons he's been calling up and the power he needs to do it."

"Is that every day?"

Des nodded.

"So if we go hunting at three, we can have nearly twenty-four hours without having to worry about demons?"

"I like the way you think." Des grinned.

"That's because you're not standing on the sidelines wondering what's happening."

"Don't tell me I've found something you actually enjoy."

"There's a lot of things I enjoy."

"Things you find pleasurable without being wracked by guilt afterwards."

"Plenty."

"Name one."

"Church."

"You've got to be joking." Des looked horrified.

"You asked."

Des shook his head. "How very sad. Name another."

"Sword training."

"Not too violent for your 'turn the other cheek' philosophy you Christians seem to believe in?"

"Oh, forget it." Scarlett tried to pull away but he continued to hold her hand.

"No parties or night clubs on your list?"

"Not night clubs."

Des laughed. "And I bet the parties are pretty tame."

"Look. This is my life. I'm not living it to please you."

"Doesn't sound like you're living it to please yourself either."

"I don't need to explain my life choices to you and why I like them and take pleasure in them. So stop trying to make me question things I'll never question." Des stared at her with an unfathomable smile on his face and the silence dragged out between them. "What?"

"Some thoughts are not meant for words."

Before Scarlett could ask what he meant, a dark sedan pulled up beside them. The window lowered and Alex glared at her.

"Looks like the cavalry has arrived. Time to run to safety." Des let her hand go.

Scarlett slowly shook her head. "Get in the back." She turned to the vehicle and opened the door. Sliding onto the front seat, she reached out to fleetingly touch her brother's arm. "See, unharmed."

He pointed to the small chiller bag on the floor at her feet. "Blake sent that." As soon as the doors were closed, Alex pulled out into the traffic.

Scarlett hurriedly buckled up and then opened the chiller bag. Inside was an ice brick and the burn ointment. She quickly put some on her new blisters and ignored the tight look on Alex's face.

The drive back to Blake's home was quiet. Several times Scarlett thought of something to say to Alex, but he looked so closed off she kept her thoughts to herself. When they stepped inside, Blake met them with a saltshaker in his hands.

"You don't have to do that yet. Not until three in the morning, or whenever you go to bed. Whichever comes first," Scarlett said.

Blake sat the salt on the floor by the door. "Dinner's ready if you three are hungry."

"I'll take mine in my room," Alex said.

"Riley will be keeping you company then." Blake looked at Alex who refused to meet his gaze. When Alex brushed past him, Blake grabbed him by the upper arm. Still Alex didn't turn to look at him. "Without this demon that you can't stand to break bread with, Scarlett would be dead. It's not up to us to judge him. That's for another. You're not being asked to be his best friend. All you have to do is show tolerance. Talk to Father Joe. It might help you clear your thoughts on the issue."

"Are you done?" Alex demanded.

Blake sighed. "Yeah." He let Alex go.

Scarlett watched her brother walk away and wanted to run after him. Before she could, Blake dropped his arm around her shoulders and guided her towards the kitchen.

"You going to tell me about the lack of demons between now and three?" Blake asked.

"You should be asking Des. I was little more than a spectator," Scarlett complained.

Blake laughed. "And how that must be annoying you."

Chapter Thirteen

Scarlett sat on the couch with her feet tucked under her and a book in her lap as her eyes stared sightlessly ahead. Her blurred view was broken by Des as he stepped in front of her. She looked up at him and noticed he wore no shirt and had a sword slung across his back.

"What's going on? Where'd you get that sword?"

Des grinned. "It's mine, I summoned it. Grab your sword."

"Why?"

"I'm curious." He held out his hand and dragged her to her feet when she took it.

She picked up her sword that had been on the couch beside her and left the book in its place, making sure she only touched the leather scabbard. "Are you going to tell me?" She walked beside him to the back door.

"How about I show you instead?" He flicked the switch to turn the spotlights on in the backyard. "Come and play."

Scarlett returned his grin. "I had planned to get an early night." She took the hand he offered and followed him to the middle of the spacious backyard. The perimeter of the yard was filled with shrubs and plants that pressed up against the wooden fence and several large trees were scattered around the edges, stretching towards the large grassed area in the middle.

"You're fooling yourself if you think you can sleep yet." Des drew his sword.

Scarlett pulled the glove from her jeans pocket and slipped it on her left hand before she drew her sword from its sheath. She tossed the leather scabbard towards the closest tree. "And you think this is going to help me sleep?"

Des shrugged. "Does it matter? At least it's better than sitting there brooding." He attacked and she blocked. "Put some effort into it, Scarlett. It's not like you can kill me."

"This is a blessed sword. A cut from it will be painful."

Des attacked again, Scarlett blocked each one, not

attacking back. "You draw blood and you can take one of the questions from me. It'll be yours to ask."

"No. I'm not hurting you."

"I'll fight you," Alex said from the back door.

"No. Alex!"

Alex shrugged at his sister's words. "He's asking for it. Are you mad, Scarlett? You can't like him. He's a demon."

Des smiled triumphantly. "You fight me or I fight your brother. And you fight to win."

"What if I lose? And what are the rules that govern my losing? You're not cutting me."

"Disarm."

Scarlett stared at him. "If I win, we're at even questions. One each."

"Done!" Des attacked immediately.

Scarlett blocked and attacked back. The sword felt a part of her, whistling through the air to clash against Des' sword. The rest of the world faded and it was only the two of them. She met his gaze and looked into his eyes for clues. There were none. She circled him and attacked randomly. He blocked each time.

Excitement rushed through her as she came close to his arm. He twisted away at the last minute and brought his sword down on hers. She had to step back to keep her grip. She grinned at him and swung high, then she changed direction at the last second. He barely managed to block.

Time became meaningless, measured by the clash of swords, the pounding of hearts and quick breaths from exertion. A trickle of sweat went down the side of her face, but Scarlett ignored it. There was no time for distractions. She went back to blocking as her shoulders started to feel the weight of the sword. They circled each other warily.

Scarlett was driven back under a barrage of attacks and she stumbled on an exposed root. Des reached out to save her as Scarlett gained her balance and attacked. He brought his sword up too late and Scarlett managed to catch his side, a line of blood instantly welling.

Des staggered and swore. Scarlett lowered her sword and wrapped her arm around him in support.

"I told you it'd hurt. And what was that? I was fine. I didn't need your help. Didn't you hassle me earlier for not playing properly?"

Des laughed. "Instinct."

Scarlett frowned. "Saving me from being hurt is instinct?"

"Apparently." He drew his breath in sharply. "What did you do to that sword? Douse it in holy water?" When she nodded, he swore again. "Now you tell me. I thought it was only blessed by your priest. I didn't know you'd dipped it in holy water too."

"You're the one who wanted to play."

"I obviously don't think clearly around you."

Scarlett met his gaze. "Neither do I," she said softly.

He leaned forward, his lips a breath away from hers.

"You better clean that blood off your sword, just in case it's corrosive," Alex called out.

Des grinned. "Saved by the bell," he murmured.

Scarlett laughed and pulled away, her gaze drawn to the cut. She reached out and ran her fingers through the blood. The wound was closed. It hadn't been very deep, but it should have taken much longer to heal.

"Scarlett! What are you doing? Finger painting?" Alex strode across the lawn to her.

"He's healed."

"He's a demon." Alex glared at Des.

Scarlett looked at the red smearing her fingers. She held them up towards her brother. "Funny how our blood is the same colour though."

"Scarlett. Don't argue with your brother over me," Des said.

"I don't need you to defend me, demon," Alex snapped.

"I'm not. I'm protecting Scarlett."

"I wouldn't harm her."

"Not physically." Des stared at Alex a moment before he turned and walked back to the house.

Alex looked sick. "I'm sorry, Scarlett." He reached out his left hand.

She had to lean her sword against her leg so she could clasp her left hand to his arm so their wrists touched. The familiar action said more than words could. It reminded both of them about what was involved in gaining their demon marks and how their family always stood together. "I'm sorry too. I know how hard you're finding this. I wish I could make it easier."

"That should be my line."

Scarlett smiled at him. "How about we share the line?"

"Sure." He reached out and took her sword. "I'll clean it for you."

"Thanks."

Alex fetched the scabbard and they walked side by side into the house. Alex moved to the sink and grabbed a rag from the cupboard beneath. He ignored Des who poured a glass of juice.

"Here." Des handed the juice to Scarlett.

She checked the clock as she drained the glass. "We were out there nearly two hours."

Des chuckled. "Think you might be able to sleep now?"

"Like the dead." She put her glass on the sink and washed the blood from her hand, watching as it swirled down the drain. Not wanting to take any chances that the blood could be used against him, she pulled the vial of holy water from her jeans pocket and tipped some down the sink before she returned the vial to her pocket. She turned back to Des who had already cleaned the blood off himself. "How do you feel?"

"Fine. It hurt a hell of a lot longer than I expected. Nasty surprise that holy water."

"I wasn't the one who decided to play." She took her sheathed sword Alex handed her. "Thanks." She turned back to Des. "You even set the rules."

"I'm not complaining. Just stating a fact."

"I'm going to bed shortly," Alex said to Scarlett. "You going?"

"Yeah. I need to shower first."

"Night, Scarlett."

"Night." Scarlett watched as Alex left the room. She was glad he was no longer angry with her, but she guessed with the way he'd ignored Des he was still unhappy with a demon in the house. She turned back to Des to find him watching her. "What?"

"I'm glad you and your brother are no longer at odds." He moved closer. "And it was worth the pain to see you have fun."

"You're mad."

Des grinned. "I see things differently to you." He took another step towards her.

Scarlett moved away a step. "I need to have a shower."

"You going to come hunting, Lady Knight?"

"It barely seems like hunting when I'm only a spectator."

"It makes it easier to send them back when you help. It would take much longer to completely defeat them. Are you coming hunting with me?"

"Yes."

"I'll wake you just before three." Des grinned before he walked outside.

Scarlett stared after him and wondered what he was up to. In the end she yawned, shrugged and went to get some clothes so she could shower.

Chapter Fourteen

"Lady Knight."

Scarlett shivered at the words whispered in her ear. She opened her eyes to see a shadow leaning over her. She reached out and her hand touched the heat of Des' skin.

"If you have other plans we can postpone the hunt."

Scarlett smiled. "And you call me predictable." Climbing out of the swag, she grabbed her phone and wallet. She stood, shoving them in the pockets of her jeans she'd been tired enough to fall asleep in. A rattle of keys in the doorway made them both turn towards the sound.

Blake stood in the doorway of the lounge room. "Looks like we're ready to go. I'm driving." He held his sword in one hand, his keys in the other.

"Scarlett?" Des asked.

"That's good. My car's still out of action."

Des took her hand and guided her through the dimly lit room. Once they were in the four-wheel-drive, that was parked in the driveway, Blake turned the key to accessories. The clock in the dash sent an eerie glow through the front of the vehicle. They sat in silence and waited for the few minutes that still had to pass before it was three o'clock.

The moment the clock changed to three, Des said, "Go left." For nearly an hour he gave Blake terse directions until he finally told him to pull over.

Scarlett looked around as she climbed out of the four-wheel-drive. They were parked in front of a building site in an industrial area. Regularly spaced spotlights created large pools of light. The street was deserted, but she guessed that would change in about an hour when daylight broke and the businesses started work for the day. The lights of the vehicle flashed as Blake locked it and they followed Des onto the building site.

Des pulled off his shirt and handed it to Scarlett.

She glanced at the shirt. "Couldn't you just make it disappear and reappear?"

Des nodded. "Why waste energy that could be used for something else? Luck?"

Scarlett couldn't help smiling. She touched her

fingers to her lips then lightly to his. "Where's the demon?"

Des laughed softly. "Coward." He turned away and looked around. "There," he pointed slightly to his left, "And there." He pointed straight ahead.

"Two," Scarlett gasped.

"Then let's get this over with." Blake drew his sword from the scabbard that was now slung across his back.

"You can have the demon straight ahead. Scarlett and I will take the one to the left," Des said.

Blake stared at Des for a moment. "Return her in one piece."

Des nodded before he strode away. Scarlett followed him, patting Blake on the shoulder in reassurance as she walked past him. She paused as Des suddenly sprouted wings and leapt into the air. It was an amazing sight Scarlett had to admit. Grace and power.

She watched as Des fought the smaller demon, it's almost skeletal body equally as quick as his. Des faltered and the skeletal demon took advantage to shove him into scaffolding. It crashed down around them. Des clutched his side where she'd cut him earlier and stumbled away from the demon who let out a manic cackle.

Scarlett started to run towards Des.

"Stay back, Scarlett."

"What's wrong?"

"Must still have holy water in my system. I thought I'd burned it all out. Your cousin's praying makes it burn like hell."

"We'll move away from him." Scarlett backed towards the street.

Des launched himself at the other demon and his momentum pushed them further away from Blake. Scarlett was on the footpath now and hurried to the corner of the street. She turned around to see if Des followed. She saw the skeletal demon point at her before Des leapt at it again.

Scarlett heard the roar of an engine off to her right and turned to see a car heading straight for her. She heard a shout from behind and as she started to move, she looked over her shoulder in time to see a leather clad man running towards her, pushing her out of the way of the car.

Everything seemed to happen in slow motion, before Scarlett hit the footpath. There was a sickening thud as the car hit the man who had saved her, tossing him aside like a rag doll. The car raced down the street without pausing to check on the man it had hit. Scarlett heard a scream and realised it was hers.

She cut it off in mid sound to hear Des frantically calling her name. She couldn't answer. Her whole being was focused on scrambling to her feet and getting to the man. She dropped to her knees beside him. He was too still. Blood stained the footpath beneath his head. One of his legs was at an unnatural angle and his chest was still.

"Please," Scarlett whispered as she pressed her fingers against his wrist to find a pulse. Nothing. She unzipped his leather jacket, which it was far too hot to be wearing, and felt for his heartbeat. Still nothing.

"No!" Scarlett frantically began CPR. She prayed as she worked and then recalled Des still fought a demon. A tear splashed on her hands as she worked on his chest and she realised she was crying. She started mouth to mouth again. Nothing.

With trembling hands, she dialled emergency and set it to speakerphone before she went back to working on the young man. As soon as she was connected, she yelled, "I need an ambulance."

She looked around hysterically when she was asked for a location and sobbed. "I don't know."

"Scarlett!" Des yelled.

She glanced up in his direction and he yelled GPS co-ordinates to her. She sobbed in relief as she passed on the information. Scarlett had no sooner disconnected the call when Des yelled out to her again.

"Scarlett! Now!"

She paused long enough to grab her cross with her left hand and braced herself for the jolt of pain. Then Des was beside her and lifting her out of the way.

"Save him," Scarlett begged.

He ran his hand over the leg and it straightened. The bleeding stopped at the back of the head. He held his hand over the heart and the forehead. He looked up at Scarlett and shook his head.

"No! Save him."

"It's too late, Scarlett. He's already gone."

Des tried to wrap his arms around Scarlett, but she struck out at him with her fists. He pulled her close. "It was too late the moment the car hit him."

"No," Scarlett sobbed. "I was the one who was meant to be hit. Not him. Me."

"Don't even think it," Des ordered. "I would rather a dozen people died than have you die."

"That's horrible." Scarlett tried to pull away from him.

"It might be. But it's the truth."

"I could have got out of the way in time if he hadn't been there," Scarlett whispered.

"No you couldn't. The demon forced that car after

you. It wouldn't have stopped until a life was taken. Someone had to die."

"We shouldn't have gone hunting."

"You think it would have been better to let them run loose and do more damage?"

Scarlett's voice broke. "They were after me, no one else."

"They would have created havoc everywhere they went while they looked for you. Conflict and Dissension. They couldn't have helped themselves."

"I don't want to be the cause of other people's pain," Scarlett whispered. She looked down at the man lying on the footpath. She pulled away from Des and felt his arms tighten before he let her go. She knelt beside the body. The man wore black jeans, motorbike boots and a leather jacket. Under it was a shirt printed with a heavy metal band. She reached out to touch his cheek. His face was angular with prominent cheekbones, a sharp jaw line, narrow nose and light brown eyes that stared at her sightlessly. His hair was close cropped and he had a row of earrings up both ears and in one eyebrow.

"You can't help him, Lady Knight."

"He looks like he was only my age. He had his whole life ahead of him."

Des lifted the man's hand and showed Scarlett the scars on his wrist. "Yet he didn't want it."

"It still doesn't make it right."

Des stared at her a moment. "Bind me to this youth, Scarlett."

"What?"

"You heard me."

"I can't." Scarlett shook her head, her mouth opened to speak again and then closed as she looked at the young man. "I can't," she whispered.

"He's dead. There's nothing more that can be done for him."

"It's a sin."

"And binding me to an object wasn't? Scarlett!"

Tears streaked down her face. "If I could, then I would. I won't take one step further down this path. Please don't ask it of me."

Des looked at the body, then back at Scarlett. "Please. Before it's too late. Before everything breaks down too much to be of use."

Scarlett could only shake her head as silent tears continued to course down her cheeks.

Des grabbed her by the arms. "I'm begging you, Lady Knight. Please."

"Don't ask this of me. Des! I can't do it. It was hard enough to bind you to the ring. This isn't necessary."

"Scarlett-"

"No. Aren't you the one who said you were averse to change? This would be a major change."

"No, it wouldn't. All that would change would be the shell. I'd still be myself. Please, Scarlett."

Scarlett shook her head. Her words were soft and broken. "I… can't."

Blake ran towards them. "Scarlett!" He dropped beside her and wrapped her in his arms. "You're unhurt?" When she could only nod in answer, he looked between her, Des and the body. "What happened?"

"He saved my life. The demon forced a car to run me over. And he saved my life. I don't even know his name." Scarlett shook her head. "I don't even know his name."

Des met Blake's gaze. "Do you want me with her forever, bound to the ring she wears on her hand? The moment I'm no longer bound to her, I'll be Retribution's plaything. I'm not a fool. Do you think I'll let her break the binding? There's another option." Des glanced at the body and then back to Blake. "It's an empty shell. Bind me to it."

"Blake! No! Don't take that path. Don't listen to him. Please."

Blake let Scarlett pull away from him. "No binding.

A soul. To become human with all the frailties that involves."

"Blake?" Scarlett looked between the two and worry filled her eyes.

Des hesitated and then looked at Scarlett. "Willingly."

"Give me the ring, Scarlett." Blake held out his hand, his gaze still on Des. "Hurry. I can hear ambulance sirens."

"No."

"We don't have time to debate the morality of it. Think of it as a heart transplant," Blake said.

"Please, Scarlett," Des pleaded when Scarlett continued to hesitate.

Blake turned to look at Scarlett. "I will have that ring, Scarlett. Now hand it over."

"This is wrong." Scarlett took the ring from her finger, giving it to Blake.

Blake shook his head. "We're giving this demon the chance to redeem himself. We'll see if he wastes the chance or not."

"You're not a priest, Blake."

Blake grinned wryly. "No, and I've never wanted to be one. But this is right. I know it is." He turned to the man lying beside him. Des moved to the other side of the body. "Is it still viable?"

Des nodded. He ran his hand over the body and paused in a few places. His eyes became flame streaked. "The damage is minimal now. I'll leave the rest for the doctors."

Blake placed his left hand on the man's forehead. He turned to Scarlett. "He's left. This body's an empty shell."

Scarlett watched the procedure. Blake seemed certain about the ethics, but she wasn't sure. She should have been worried about the life that had been lost, but what bothered her most was Des' chance of survival. He was a demon. She should be glad he might not live through this. But she wasn't.

Blake turned to Des. "You will be the man. You will be human. Your soul will be judged at the end of your days. Even if those are only moments from now because the body might not survive or it rejects you."

"I know the risks. I welcome them." Des again looked towards Scarlett. When his gaze met hers, he mouthed the words, Lady Knight.

Scarlett pressed her hands to her mouth and tried to hold back the sobs that threatened to weaken her. She watched as Blake slipped her ring onto the lifeless hand, the gold stretching to fit. He then pressed his hand against the dead man's heart while his other hand went to the same place on Des.

"Are you willing to take on the responsibilities and obligations this body has left behind? To become him?"

"Yes."

"Do you renounce being a demon? Do you willingly give it up to become human?"

"With all my being."

"Do you renounce Satan and wish to find forgiveness for all the sins you have committed in the past?"

"Yes."

The air seemed to pulse and shimmer, then Des was no more.

"No," Scarlett sobbed, reaching out to touch the body. She stopped at the last second. "Tell me he lives. Please tell me he lives."

"He lives."

"Thank you, God. Thank you," Scarlett whispered and crossed herself before she placed her head on his chest to hear for herself.

The ambulance pulled up near them and two men rushed towards them with a gurney. "Make room," one of them called out. A third man joined them, bringing the equipment he needed to save the injured man's life.

Scarlett watched as the three men from the

ambulance worked over Des. When they had him on the gurney and were starting to wheel him away, Scarlett leapt forward. "Please. Take me too."

"And you are?" One of the men asked while the other two put Des in the ambulance.

"He saved my life. There was a car. I just need to thank him. Please. Can I come too?"

"I'm sorry. You're not family," the man said gently. "You're welcome to go to the hospital. Once he's stable you'll probably be able to see him. It won't be today though."

"Which hospital?" When they told her, Scarlett wailed, "But I don't even know his name."

"We found his license." One of the men called from inside the ambulance. "Jesse Finley."

"We have to go." The man turned and hurried to the driver's seat.

Scarlett buried her face in her hands. "What have we done?"

Blake dropped his arm around her shoulders and drew her close. "It'll be fine, Scarlett. Shh. Let me take you home. You'll feel better then."

"Can we go by the church first? I need to talk to Father Joe."

"Later. You look like you're about to collapse. Have a rest first."

Scarlett smiled weakly. "Okay. Home then. But do you think he'll go and see Des for me? See if things are..." her voice trailed off as she searched for the words she needed.

"To see that he's human and not a demon?"

"Yes."

"What did you think?"

"I saw what I wanted to see."

"I saw what was true. But he'll visit Jesse if that's what you want him to do. You know he's always there for us. We only have to ask."

"But he can't sense demons like we can," Scarlett said the words she knew her cousin was thinking as she touched the demon mark on her wrist.

"No. But he'll go anyway. Just to set your mind at ease."

"Good. I think I need that."

"Come on. I can hear police sirens. I know we shouldn't be leaving like this, but what can we tell them? A demon attacked Jesse?"

They ran to the vehicle and Blake pulled out onto the street. He drove sedately away while Scarlett glanced out the back window.

Chapter Fifteen

After an hour of trying to sleep, Scarlett gave up and went to knock on Blake's bedroom door. "Blake?"

"Yeah, come in."

She opened the door to see him yawn as he sat up in bed. "I can't sleep. Can we go to the hospital? I really need to see Des."

Blake yawned again. "They probably won't let you in this early."

"I don't care."

He silently watched her for a moment before he nodded and climbed out of bed. "Go get ready. I'll only be a few minutes. And Scarlett, start thinking of him as Jesse. That's who he is now."

They picked up Alyssa on the way to the hospital and she was fascinated by their night, even though Blake reminded her a young man had lost his life.

Blake dropped Scarlett at the front door of the

hospital while he and Alyssa went to find an empty car park. She walked to the counter and asked about Jesse Finley.

"And who are you?" The woman sitting at the computer asked.

"Scarlett Hunter."

"Are you family?"

"No. But I really need to see him. I need to make sure he's okay."

The woman shook her head sympathetically. "I'm sorry, but unless you're family or have the permission of his family, you can't see him."

"How is he? Will he be okay?"

"You'll have to ask the immediate family."

"Excuse me."

Scarlett spun around to see who had tapped her on her shoulder. "Yes?"

The man, who looked like he hadn't slept all night if the bags under his sharp blue eyes were anything to go by, flashed a badge at her. "Detective Tuck. Did you say you were Scarlett Hunter?"

"Yes." Scarlett wished she'd waited and not been so impatient.

"I know some Hunters, I don't suppose you'd be related to them?"

Scarlett forced a smile. "What are their first names? It's always possible. My family's very large."

"Now that is a problem. Never found out." He smiled wryly. "I don't suppose you know anything about the car that hit the Finley kid."

Scarlett was startled by the sudden question. "I wish I did. It doesn't seem right someone isn't charged over it. I'm Jesse's friend. Can you tell me how he is? Do you know when he'll be able to have visitors?"

"Hospitals don't make that sort of information available to just anyone. Although if you were related to the Hunter family that I know, I could vouch for you," Tuck said.

Scarlett stared at him. She wanted to open her mouth and admit the truth. But she couldn't do that to her family. She waited until she'd smothered the urge to say she was before she spoke again. "You can't imagine how much I want to say yes. I really need to see him. To know he'll live."

"I'm sorry. I can't help you." He handed her a familiar business card. "Let me know if you hear anything." He turned to go and ran into Blake and Alyssa.

"Blake, this is Detective Tuck," Scarlett said hurriedly.

Blake nodded and held out his hand.

"I don't suppose you know anything about the car that hit the Finley kid?"

Blake shook his head.

"Not very talkative are you?"

Blake shrugged and smiled slightly.

Alyssa threaded her arm through Blake's. "I like the strong silent type." She grinned.

"Are you two from the Hunter family too?"

"Only Blake," Scarlett answered. She looked at Blake and mouthed 'what is going on', before Tuck turned back to face her. She saw Blake mouth the word 'voice' as soon as the detective no longer looked at him. Scarlett stared at Tuck and wondered if that was why he'd questioned her. She'd certainly spoken to him on the phone many times so it was possible he'd recognised her voice. She hadn't even considered that.

"Did you get to see your boyfriend, Scarlett?" Alyssa asked.

Scarlett shook her head. "Only immediate family can visit."

"How unfair," Alyssa wailed.

"It would be unfair to the family to let some random person off the street wander in and see the kid," Tuck said. "If you're his girlfriend, I'm sure his father will let you in to see him when he arrives."

At Blake's confused expression, Scarlett explained, "He's under the impression we might be related to a family he knows by the name of Hunter. A family he trusts enough that he'd be willing to arrange for me to see Jesse." She saw the anger Blake fought to contain.

"Scarlett-"

She interrupted Blake. "I'm sure he has some little test in mind to make sure I don't lie just to be able to see Jesse."

"Some decisions can have long reaching repercussions, detective," Blake said softly.

"Are you threatening me?" Tuck demanded.

Blake shook his head. "You'd bend the rules for my cousin if she was of the correct Hunter family. And yet because you don't think she's from the right family she isn't worth the effort. What could it hurt for her to see him? You can escort her there and back. Five minutes isn't much to ask."

"I have other things to do than babysit some kid," Tuck said.

"And how would she know what to say to prove she was from the correct family? Have you given her a name maybe to ask if she knows them?" Blake persisted.

"No names. But all it would take is one word. And

she'd know what that word would be if she was from that family. Call if you can help me with the car who hit the boy." Tuck started to turn away.

"Hell of a way to treat a girl who's desperate to know how her boyfriend fares. Even the devil himself wouldn't be so cruel," Blake said, his voice still very soft.

Tuck slowly turned to face Blake. "Are you trying to tell me something?"

"Only that you're being uncharitable and unchristian to a person who may one day be in a position to help you," Blake said.

"Blake," Scarlett reached out and put her hand on his arm. "Don't worry about it. I'll sit over there in one of those chairs," she gestured towards them, "and check every hour until they say he can have visitors other than family."

Tuck didn't take his gaze off Blake, he acted like Scarlett hadn't spoken. "If you have something to tell me, don't speak about it in riddles."

"Only what everyone who has read the story of the lion and the mouse knows. Help often comes from the most unlikely of sources. Think of it as your Good Samaritan deed for the day."

Tuck's eyes narrowed. "I don't like riddles."

"And I don't like people who wield their authority

like it's a power. I tend to want to avoid them. Permanently."

Tuck looked at each of them. Blake stood in the middle with Alyssa and Scarlett on each side of him. He glanced at the demon mark that wound its way up Blake's arm to just past his elbow. "What's the meaning of that? Is it a gang mark?" He looked at Scarlett and Alyssa's wrists.

"Blake." Scarlett pleaded. Her family was more important than her need to see Jesse. Or at least it should be. A part of her didn't want to stop him.

"You have to face your demons to get one of these marks," Blake said.

Scarlett couldn't believe Blake had spoken the word Tuck was waiting to hear. She wanted to make him take it back, but couldn't think of any way to do so without drawing more attention to it.

Alyssa giggled nervously. "Their family has a tradition of lengthening the mark for every important milestone they pass. Or what the family thinks of as important milestones."

"Demons." Tuck continued to stare at Blake.

Blake grinned. "Metaphorically speaking of course. Aren't demons fairytales told to keep children in line?"

"Five minutes. And you two wait here." Tuck pointed first to Blake and then to Alyssa.

"Thank you, Detective." Blake said.

Tuck's eyes narrowed, but he didn't say anything. He turned to Scarlett. "Hurry up. Before his father gets here and wants to know what you're doing in his son's room."

Scarlett followed the detective to the elevator. "No one's been to see him yet?" When he shook his head she closed her eyes for a second and thought of the hours Des… Jesse had been alone. "Why hasn't anyone come to be with him?"

"No one's been able to track down his father. He's not at home and isn't due at work for about another hour. There's no other family."

"How…" Scarlett cleared her throat and tried again. "How's he doing?"

"Not good. He seems to be fading before their eyes and they're not sure what's wrong."

Scarlett swallowed hard. She was about to ask another question when the elevator opened and a couple entered. She fell silent. Another two stops for more people to hop on and then Tuck ushered her out of the elevator. He led her down an almost empty corridor and the sound of their footsteps echoed around them. Tuck opened a door and gestured for Scarlett to enter.

She froze in the doorway and her hands covered her mouth, one on the other. She took three hesitant steps forward and her legs felt like they would give out from under her. He looked so small with all the machines, cords and tubes. And he was nearly as white as the sheets.

"Only five minutes," Tuck reminded her.

Scarlett nodded her head and choked back a sob that threatened to escape. She forced her legs to carry her to his side and took his left hand in hers. All his jewellery had been removed, including the ring. She looked frantically around for it. Moving to the set of drawers beside the bed, she opened it. There it was, tangled with his earrings.

"What are you doing?" Tuck came into the room.

Scarlett ignored him and slid the ring back on Jesse's finger, relieved to see it still fit whoever wore it. She bent forward and pressed her lips to his forehead. Then she moved her head until her mouth was near his ear. "Wake up, Jesse. Please. Des! Open your eyes now. You're scaring me." A tear dripped down her face to land on Jesse's cheek. "Des, you said you'd protect me. Who's going to protect me when you're lying in this bed?"

"Scarlett?"

Scarlett pulled back to see dark eyes looking at her. She laughed, giddy with relief. An alarm went off and a nurse bustled into the room to check on Jesse. The nurse tried to move Scarlett out of the way.

"No!" Jesse tried to sit up and the alarm the nurse had turned off started again. "Scarlett."

"I'm here, Jesse. I'm not going anywhere." She clung to his hand and the nurse moved around to the other side of the bed.

"You're Scarlett?" The nurse asked.

Scarlett nodded.

"We thought he was talking about the colour of the blood. One of the doctors said it was all gone and that was the last he spoke. I'm glad you came in. You're just what he needed," the nurse said. "Are you able to stick around for a while? It'd do him a world of good if you could. A patient's recovery can be sped up by their desire to heal."

Scarlett looked over to Tuck. He nodded and headed for the door. Scarlett turned back to the nurse. "I have family waiting downstairs for me. Can someone give them a message that I'll be staying for a while?"

"Sure thing, love. Here, let me pull a chair over for

you." The nurse dragged one of the visitor chairs over and put it close to the bed.

Scarlett dropped thankfully into it. The moment the nurse had left, she rested her head on the bed, her left hand wrapped around Jesse's. Within seconds she had fallen asleep sitting there with her head still on the bed.

The sound of the door opening jolted her awake. She blinked and tried to focus on the large man who filled the doorway. Light brown eyes glittered in anger, knuckles white where they gripped the door, the other hand clenched into a fist. He wore a high visibility work shirt, navy shorts, had a neat trimmed beard and hair as short as Jesse's.

"Who are you and what are you doing here? On second thought, I couldn't care less. Just get out. I'm sick of all of you. Ever since Jess started hanging out with you lot, he's been permanently in trouble."

"I'm n-"

"Out. Now! Before I call someone to throw you out."

Scarlett rose reluctantly to her feet. She tucked Jesse's arm under the sheets then turned and lightly kissed his forehead. "I'll be back as soon as possible," she whispered. She walked towards the door and waited for the man to get out of the way. There were enough similarities in looks for her to know this man was Jesse's father.

He shifted to the side and continued to glare at Scarlett until she'd walked past him. Scarlett turned back when she heard the door close. She stood in the middle of the corridor and stared at it. Jesse's father had to leave at some stage, but how was she to know when that would be? As badly as she wanted to stand in the corridor and wait for him to leave, she forced herself to walk to the elevator and press the button. When the door pinged open, she pushed the ground floor button then leaned against the back wall, closing her eyes. She was so tired. She'd go home first and have a sleep. Maybe then she'd be able to think clearer.

Chapter Sixteen

Scarlett stared at the angry man who blocked Jesse's room, Blake stood in the corridor behind her. She had managed to avoid Jesse's father for the past five days, sneaking in late at night so she didn't run into him. "I–"

"You're not welcome here. And I'm guessing this is yours." He held the ring out to her.

Scarlett took it, her mouth opened to speak. Nothing came out. Her eyes filled with tears. "He has to–"

"They told me you put it on him. That you've been sneaking in here around midnight every night this week. If you keep visiting I'll take a restraining order out on you."

Fear rushed in on her. How was she meant to help Jesse survive? "But you don't und–"

"That's my son in there." He gestured towards the

room. "My son! And to put that ring on him like you're married. I don't know what game you're playing, but my boy's fighting for his life."

"I know–"

"You don't know anything. They said he might not make it through the night. He's had a relapse. So don't keep coming around here pushing yourself in where you're not wanted."

Anger made her hands curl into fists as he interrupted every comment she tried to make. "Was that before or after the ring was removed?" Scarlett was amazed she actually managed to get a full sentence out, but her anger didn't lessen.

"That's none of your business. Now get out of here before I ask the staff to call the cops."

Blake came to stand beside Scarlett. "Come on. Time to go, Scarlett. You're wasting your time here. We could light a candle for Jesse in the chapel."

"But, Blake," Scarlett wailed.

"Scarlett. Now." Blake's eyes pleaded with her to follow his lead.

Scarlett sagged against him. She didn't want to take one step away from Jesse. She wanted to push past his father and run to his side. How could Blake expect her to walk off without trying to see him? Without trying to save him.

"You're trying my patience," Jesse's father growled.

Blake took a step away and tried to get Scarlett to follow him. She wouldn't budge. "Scarlett. Be sensible. Jesse's father has the right to deny you entrance to his room. Come to the chapel and light a candle for him." When Scarlett shook her head, Blake sighed heavily. "You move on your own or I throw you over my shoulder and drag you away from here. What's it going to be?"

Scarlett gasped at Blake's tone. "Blake?" How could he fail her? He was family. They were meant to stick together.

"That's an order," he said firmly.

Scarlett pulled away from him and strode away from Jesse's room, fuming. Turning right at the next corridor she gasped as Blake grabbed her by the arm and pulled her into a room marked 'Staff Only'. She pushed him away from her.

"How could you?" Tears stained her cheeks and anger gleamed in her eyes.

Blake pulled out his phone. "You won't have long. You'd better make the most of it."

"What?" Scarlett frowned as her anger started to evaporate, replaced by confusion.

"Can I speak to Thomas Finley, please?" Blake rattled off Jesse's floor and room number. "Could you page him to the nurses' station so the phone doesn't disturb the patient? Thank you."

"Blake?" Scarlett's mind struggled to go from devastating pain back to hope.

Blake grinned at her when they heard Thomas being paged. He held up a hand to stop her when she was about to rush out. He pressed mute on his phone. "Give him a moment."

"How did you know his name?"

"What else have I got to do other than read Jesse's charts while you're busy holding his hand and staring intently at him?"

Scarlett threw her arms around her cousin. "I love you." She couldn't stop grinning.

"Yeah well, a little more faith in me earlier would have helped."

"I'm sorry. I wasn't thinking clearly."

"I hope you're thinking clearer now. Go to him, Scarlett. I'll pray you can help him."

Scarlett swiftly kissed him on the cheek and then opened the door enough to check the corridor. It was clear. She hurried back to Jesse's room. Her heart pounded loudly. The door was closed. Holding her breath, she reached out to open it. Only Jesse was in the room. She ran to his side and pushed her ring back on his finger.

"Jesse. Please. Oh, Des, don't you dare leave me. I need you here." She clasped his hand in hers. "Des. Talk to me. Tell me you're still there. I won't let you leave. Do you hear me?" Tears ran freely down her cheeks. "Please," she whispered. She should have fought Blake harder. Des was going to die and it was all her fault.

She stared at the monitors that were hooked up to him, but they meant nothing to her. Sniffing, she checked in her pockets for a tissue. Instead she found Des' feather. She looked at the small, soft feather then down at Jesse. It was all that was left of his demon self and belonged to him. She pressed it into his left hand and curled her hand around his to hold it between them. The feather moved and brushed against the ring. There was a flash of light, extreme pain shot through her hand and then alarms went off on monitors.

Gasping, Scarlett clutched the rails of the bed to steady herself until the pain subsided. She reached out for Jesse's hand again only to stop. Curving from the base of his palm towards his thumb was what looked like a black feather tattooed on him, the real one gone. She gingerly reached out and touched his palm. When nothing happened, she clasped his hand to her.

Two medical staff burst into the room and brushed

Scarlett out of the way. Another entered and went to the monitors. Everything fell silent until Blake burst into the room minutes later. He halted when he saw the crowd in the room. He cautiously entered and the look in his eyes sent warnings to Scarlett.

She turned to the closest person and read the name badge. "Doctor Penfoll, is he going to be okay?"

The doctor smiled at her wearily. "You're the best medicine he could have at the moment. Every time you visit with him his vital signs improve. Part of medicine is in the patient's mind. He needs to want to recover."

"No!" Thomas bellowed from the doorway. "I don't want her near him."

Doctor Penfoll sighed heavily. "That is of course up to you Mr Finley. But if you want your son to recover, like you say you do, I'd make this girl sit at his bedside every second of the day."

Thomas sagged visibly. He moved out of the way to let the rest of the staff out. Only Doctor Penfoll stayed in the room. He waited patiently for Thomas to make his decision. No one else spoke and Scarlett could barely bring herself to breathe.

"Scarlett." The single word from Jesse made Scarlett run to his side and grasp his hand again.

"I'm here. I'm here." She pressed his hand against her cheek. "Just don't go."

"Scarlett." Her name was a relieved whisper.

Thomas staggered into the room to sit heavily on one of the visitor chairs. When Doctor Penfoll started to move towards him, he waved him away and his head fell into his hands. Doctor Penfoll hesitated and then, with one last look around the room, left.

Minutes passed as Scarlett stood by Jesse's side and clung to his hand, Blake stood against the wall and Thomas sat with his head buried in his hands while the occasional shudder tore through him. He eventually rose to his feet and stumbled to the door.

"Scarlett," Blake called out.

Scarlett looked over to her cousin who nodded towards Thomas as he opened the door. "Mr Finley."

He turned to face her, his cheeks damp, his eyes underlined by shadows. "He needs you more than he does me."

Scarlett shook her head. "He needs you too." She couldn't say what was really in her mind. That Thomas needed to be by Jesse's side possibly more than she needed to be there. Guilt tugged at her that it wasn't Thomas' Jesse in the bed.

Thomas shook his head. "No. He hasn't needed me for years. I hardly know him. We share a house and occasionally run into each other. Barely housemates. I don't even know who his friends are anymore. I didn't even know you existed."

Sorrow mixed with the guilt she felt. "Then keep me company. It gets very lonely sitting here waiting for him to talk." She tried for a lighter tone and half succeeded. "Has he always been so terrible at holding up his end of the conversation?"

Thomas smiled weakly. "Ever since he became a teenager. I kept hoping he'd grow out of it."

Blake brought a chair over to Scarlett so she could sit down and put another on the other side of the bed. Thomas sat silently and his gaze fell on his son, eventually being drawn to the ring. His lips tightened.

"He's too young to marry. He's at uni. Not doing very well though. Too many parties and not enough study."

"It hasn't anything to do with marriage." She tried to think of a way to describe the binding without sounding crazy or scaring Thomas. "It's has to do with promises and being responsible to yourself and those in your life," Scarlett said.

Thomas met Scarlett's gaze. "Responsible. He certainly needs to know the meaning of that word. I've worried about him a lot in the past few months."

Scarlett's gaze was drawn to the scars on Jesse's wrists that Thomas stared at. She brushed her thumb over one of the scars. Looking up, she saw Thomas watching her. "His dark days are behind him." She smiled reassuringly. "He has friends who care what he does with his life now, Mr Finley." Maybe he wasn't Thomas' Jesse, but that didn't mean he couldn't be. And wasn't it better than Thomas being without Jesse? She didn't know. Her feelings about the situation were torn in a million different directions.

"Thank you. And call me Tom. You're Scarlett, right?" When Scarlett nodded, he began to turn towards Blake.

"Blake," Scarlett called out sharply when she looked up to see he was putting salt along the window ledge. He turned to face the room, the shaker behind him. "Blake, this is Jesse's father Tom. Tom, my cousin Blake." Scarlett guessed Blake had put the saltshaker in his back pocket because she couldn't see it when he took a couple of steps forward to offer his hand to Thomas.

The door opened and Alex stepped in, a roll of white electrical tape in his hands. It disappeared into his pocket as Thomas turned towards him. "Scarlett?" Alex looked from Scarlett to Thomas.

"Tom, this is my brother Alex. Alex, this is Jesse's father Tom."

Alex stared at Scarlett for a moment before he came forward to shake Thomas' hand. "How are you coping, sir?"

Thomas smiled. "A lot better since he spoke. My boy spoke. He's got to pull through this."

Alex nodded. "You must be relieved."

"Yes. I guess you know this isn't the first time I've had to sit by his bed and wonder how much longer he'll live." Thomas glanced back towards Jesse's wrists. "It's just him and me. Has been since he was two and his mother walked out on us. I don't know what I'd do without him. He might pretend I don't exist half the time, but I know he exists. And that's important to me."

Alex's lips thinned and he turned away after a glare at Scarlett. He moved to Blake's side and quickly gave him the roll of electrical tape. He turned back to Thomas. "I hope he recovers for your sake. I might see you next time I'm here." He turned to Scarlett. "Gran said to tell you she's praying for him. Now."

Scarlett smiled slightly. Des certainly wouldn't have wanted their prayers when he'd been a demon. "Tell her, thank you. I'm sure he appreciates it... now." Alex made it to the door, before Scarlett called out, "Alex." She waited until he faced her. "I'm sorry, Alex. But I've learned life isn't a clear choice between good and evil, right and wrong. I don't regret any of my choices." She might not regret them, but she was still torn that a boy had lost his life and Des struggled to live.

"That's between you and God. What do you want from me? Forgiveness?" Alex asked.

Scarlett shook her head. "Understanding." She smiled sadly when he didn't speak. "Love you."

Alex strode back to her side and pressed a kiss to her forehead. "Always, Scarlett. No matter your choices. Just don't expect me to agree with them if I think they're wrong."

He left the room before Scarlett could say another word. She turned to see Thomas staring at her. She shrugged. "Guess you can't always see eye to eye on everything with your family." She looked towards Blake who was behind Thomas' back. He held up the electrical tape and saltshaker before he shoved them in his pockets, pointing towards the door. The electrical tape was the only way they could keep a line of salt in front of the door.

Blake strode across the room, pausing at the door. "I'll be back in a couple of hours to pick you up,

Scarlett. Nice to meet you, Tom, even under the circumstances."

Scarlett and Thomas both nodded before they returned to their vigil. They spoke very little. Scarlett continued to hold Jesse's hand and prayed that the body would finally stop trying to reject the new soul. Thomas sat and stared at his son or paced restlessly in the small room.

Chapter Seventeen

When Blake arrived to collect Scarlett, he carried a latched rectangular case with a handle. It looked like it could be some type of musician's case. Scarlett was surprised to see it. They carried their swords in the case when they needed to transport them through public places.

Scarlett rose to her feet, tucked Jesse's arm under the sheet and bent to kiss his forehead. "I'll be back later, Jesse." The word 'Des' echoed in her mind. "Wait for me. Don't go anywhere. I really need you to wait for me." She stared at him a moment longer before she turned to Thomas. "Do you mind if I return in the morning?"

Thomas shook his head. "Any time you want to sit by his side you can. I'm sorry about-"

Scarlett interrupted him. "It's okay. You don't have

to apologise for protecting your son. You didn't know who I was."

"I should have let you speak. Heard what you had to say instead of throwing you out."

"You're under a lot of strain."

"And you're too understanding."

Scarlett smiled slightly. "Not always. But I'm working on it." She moved to stand beside Blake.

"Make sure you get some sleep, Tom. You can't work on a construction site when you're sleep deprived," Blake said.

"Construction site?" Scarlett looked between the two men.

Thomas nodded. "That's why Jess was where he was when the car hit him. I'd talked my boss into giving him a trial. I thought if he had something to do while he waited for uni to start again he might not get into as much trouble. I don't know why he was there so early. I can't-"

"Don't blame yourself, Tom," Blake interrupted. "You can't see the future. You can only do the best you can with what you know and trust that God will take care of the rest."

Thomas shook his head. "Haven't believed in him much since my wife walked out on me. Actually, it was her walking out on Jess that was the hardest to understand." He glanced back at Jesse. "And sleep? Won't have time to now. I've got to leave in about an hour to get ready for work. I wish I could call in sick, but well, I've used up all my sick days and holidays the last two times he was in hospital."

"Give me a minute." Blake handed the sword case to Scarlett and stepped out of the room. The door closed softly behind him.

"What's he doing?" Thomas asked.

Scarlett shrugged. "I don't know exactly, but he'll have a solution."

"How did Jesse get lucky enough to meet you and your family?"

Scarlett was saved from having to answer the question by Blake entering the room, Riley on his heels.

"This is my brother, Riley. He'll come back in an hour to sit with Jesse."

"I–" Thomas cleared his throat. "I don't know what to say."

Riley grinned. "Thank you is usually the accepted phrase."

"Yes. Of course. Thank you. But I don't understand why you're doing this."

"No offence Tom, but I'm doing it for Scarlett. I know she won't sleep and be back here before she should. She'd have been here every minute you weren't this past week if more of the nurses had been willing to turn a blind eye to her presence. If you can give permission for the Hunter family to visit we'll make sure there's always someone to sit with him," Riley said.

"Thank you. You can't imagine how hard it's been to go to work and know he's here alone. There's no other family, well, not that I can call on anyway," Thomas said.

Riley nodded. "We'd better go otherwise I won't be back before you leave. I have something I've got to take care of first." He glanced at the case Scarlett held.

Blake took the case from Scarlett. "I'll see you later, Tom. I'd suggest having a sleep after work before you come back. No point being on the road anymore than you have to be when you're tired. We don't need you in the room next to your son."

Thomas nodded. "Thanks. I will."

When they were in the elevator, alone, Scarlett looked from her brother to her cousins. "What's happened? Why the swords?"

"There's a demon in the car park. He can't get into the room since we've kept the entrances salted, so he's waiting by the vehicle for you," Blake said.

Scarlett sighed. She just wanted to go home and sleep. To the home Gran had bought for the four of them to share. "What sort of demon?"

"Still in the lower ranks," Blake said.

Scarlett nodded. "I don't think I could cope with anything stronger at the moment."

Alex dropped an arm around her shoulders. "You've got to get more sleep."

"I know. But I can't. Not until I know Jesse's going to live. I keep dreaming I'm at his funeral. I know you don't like him Alex, but if he died…" Scarlett swallowed and tried again. "If he died–" Her voice broke on the word and she shook her head, unable to speak. If he died she'd have two deaths on her conscience and one of those deaths would haunt her for life.

Alex pulled Scarlett close and wrapped both his arms around her. "I'm sorry, Scarlett. I'll take a turn watching over him for you."

"You don't need to."

"Yes, I do." Alex smiled wryly. "You should have said something earlier. You know how stubbornly I hold onto ideas."

"A piece of four by four might have got through to him better than talking," Riley suggested.

"Ha ha, very funny," Alex muttered.

Riley grinned. "I know." He took a bow. "Comedian extraordinaire at your service."

The elevator door opened and they stepped into the corridor, headed towards the walkway that connected the hospital to the multi storey parking. Their footsteps echoed loudly in the empty walkway. As they stepped into the car park, the heat hit them.

"Looks like it's going to be another scorching day," Riley said.

"Hot as hell," Alex muttered as they walked towards the up ramp. "But what else can you expect in January?"

"Where are we parked?" Scarlett asked.

"Next level up. Halfway along," Blake answered.

"Shouldn't we take our swords out?" Scarlett looked towards the case Blake still carried.

He shook his head. "Security cameras."

"Then how are we meant to deal with the demon?" Scarlett tried to spot the cameras.

Blake grinned. "I've got that all under control."

Scarlett nodded as she walked up the ramp and looked cautiously around. The demon couldn't be too far away, she could feel the heat in her demon mark. She automatically rubbed against the warmth in her wrist.

When they reached the next level, she saw the

demon beside Blake's four-wheel-drive. He looked like a body builder on steroids. A nearly seven-foot tall body builder. Scarlett stared at the muscles that bulged and was glad fights with demons weren't always physical. She hoped this one wasn't, he looked like he could take them all on with one arm tied behind his back. Maybe even two arms tied and a blindfold. He waited with hands on his hips, his gaze fixed on them.

As soon as they were close enough, Blake called out, "There are security cameras in here, demon. We'll have plenty of help to deal with you soon enough."

The demon clapped his hands together and there was a crackle in the air. "Not anymore, human."

Blake grinned and opened the sword case. Scarlett, Riley and Alex took their swords as Blake handed them out, slinging them onto their backs. Blake snapped the case closed and leaned it against a concrete column before he slid the strap of his scabbard over his head and put one arm through it.

The demon brought his hands together again and this time a sword appeared in them. "You have no chance of surviving, humans."

"What should we call you, demon?" Blake asked as they strode forward, side-by-side.

"Feud." The demon struck at Blake who was slightly in the lead. The rest of them fanned out to circle Feud. Now they were closer, Scarlett could smell the demon. This one smelt of smouldering fire, the more powerful ones smelt worse.

The demon whirled, his sword a blur in the air as he attacked them, one after the other. Scarlett's arms vibrated with the impact. No matter how quickly they attacked, his sword was there to meet them. A blur of light. Block, attack, parry. It was a deadly dance that consumed all their concentration.

"Riley," Blake called. "Retreat. Pray." The ring of metal against metal punctuated his words.

Riley blocked an attack and leapt backwards, the gap he left reduced by Scarlett and Alex. Feud tried to follow him, but he was forced to defend himself from the three that still surrounded him.

Riley's voice rose as he started to pray. His words kept time with the clash of swords and his voice was strong as he called for help to send Feud home. Minutes passed. Minutes that slowed as they fought to protect Riley from Feud. The demon knew Riley was their best chance to end the battle. Already the prayers caused his attacks to slow and occasionally falter.

Feud stared directly at Riley, his sword still in

motion. "When I am called again, I will deal with you after I have completed my task." He parried Scarlett's sword then threw his own at Riley who dropped to the ground, his voice steady. Feud brought his hands together and there was a crackle in the air and all the overhead lights on their level broke in a shower of glass, plunging the car park into semi darkness.

They surrounded Riley who was on his feet again, their swords held ready. Scarlett felt a sword come for her, a whistle through the air. Instinct kicked in and she blocked. She guessed Feud had either called his sword back to him or materialised another one. Next she heard Alex grunt at the force of Feud's sword connecting with his. Then there was a flash of light followed by silence.

Scarlett breathed deep. The smell of demon was gone. She sheathed her sword and reached out to her family. Her hand wrapped around her brother's forearm. His hand momentarily rested on hers before he moved towards the four-wheel-drive. Blake collected the sword case and Scarlett made her way to the vehicle, Riley beside her. None of them talked in the semi-darkness. They worked together silently. Blake took each of their swords and returned them to the case he had put on the bonnet.

The vehicle's lights flashed as it was unlocked and

Alex put the key in the ignition and turned it to accessories so he could use the headlights to cut through the shadows. He grabbed two bottles of water and handed one to Scarlett. She gratefully had a drink before she handed it to Riley, glad that most demons couldn't come and go from hell whenever they wanted. Riley would be safe from Feud for a time. He was likely to be more selective of which calls he accepted so he could be certain of going after Riley. She dropped onto the backseat and her eyes closed on a sigh.

Blake brushed her hair away from her forehead. "We'll be home soon and you can sleep."

Scarlett smiled weakly, half opening her eyes. "How long do you think Nathan will keep this up?"

"We'll always stand beside you," Blake said solemnly.

Scarlett sighed. "That's what I thought. I might as well be in Europe constantly fighting demons with our parents."

"We'll find Nathan. He can't hide forever. I rang Tuck and told him to be on the lookout for him. To bring him in however possible, even if it's only for a few hours. I also gave him a mobile phone number for one of the uncles who can be at the police station within minutes so someone can be there to follow Nathan when he leaves."

"And then what do we do to stop him from calling more demons to replace the ones we send back? Cut his tongue out?"

"Scarlett–"

"Sorry, Blake. I guess I'm tired."

"We'll get you home then." Blake rested his hand on her shoulder.

"Blake."

About to turn away from Scarlett, Blake paused. "Yes?"

"What happened when you called Tuck?"

"He was full of questions. He understands now that if we wanted him to know who we are, we wouldn't ring him anonymously. I told him it's for the protection of our family that we don't want him to figure out who we are. We could always find someone else to pass our information along to. He wasn't happy and tried to argue he wouldn't put us at risk. He finally agreed to stop trying to discover exactly who we are. I guess we'll find out soon enough."

"Are we going?" Alex asked.

Scarlett chuckled when she realised Alex had beaten Blake to the driver's seat. "Guess you're passenger." She yawned when Blake shook his head, muttered that it was his vehicle, and hopped in the front passenger seat.

Riley grabbed his backpack off the seat beside Scarlett. "I don't know about you lot, but I'm out of here. I'll see you later." His gaze fell on Scarlett. "I'll look after him as I would you."

"Thank you. I owe you."

Riley shook his head with a grin. "We're family. You don't owe me anything. Just get some sleep before you collapse."

Scarlett nodded and watched as Riley swung the backpack over his shoulder, striding back the way they'd come.

Chapter Eighteen

"Scarlett."

Scarlett rose from her chair, putting aside the book she'd been reading, and bent close so she could hear Jesse's whispers. "I'm here."

"So tired, Scarlett. I can't stop sleeping."

Scarlett smiled. "I know. Your body needs it to heal."

"I didn't-"

"Jesse. Your Dad's here too." She spoke quickly, worried Jesse might say something Thomas shouldn't hear. She looked over to Thomas who stood up and moved closer.

Jesse stared at Thomas with a frown. He looked back to Scarlett. "I don't know him."

Thomas recoiled like he'd been struck.

Scarlett gripped Jesse's hand tighter, wanting to demand what he was doing. "You must. He's your

Dad." Don't do this, she wanted to say. Tell him you know him, he's desperate to be acknowledged by you.

"The only thing I recall is talking to you. That's it. Walking along a street and talking to you. And a car coming towards me. Two separate memories. The rest is blank. And the name Jesse doesn't mean anything to me. The only name I know is yours."

Scarlett looked towards Thomas who seemed frozen. Her heart ached for him and she wanted to hit Jesse and tell him not to be so cruel.

"Where did he go?" Jesse asked.

"Who?" The anger she felt made the word sharp.

"My father. I can't see anything lying here like this. Help me sit up."

"You can't. You were hit by a car," Scarlett protested. "You're supposed to be resting." He obviously didn't understand what it meant to be human.

"Where's my father, Scarlett?"

Scarlett looked over to Thomas. He still looked devastated. "He's here."

"I can't see him."

"Tom?" Scarlett stared at the shell-shocked man.

He took a hesitant step forward. Then another.

One slow step at a time until he was in Jesse's view. "I'm here." His voice was barely more than a whisper.

Jesse looked at Thomas. "I don't know you." He smiled wryly. "I don't even know me. All I know is Scarlett. I'm sorry, Dad."

At the last three words, a shudder went through Thomas. "Jess, it'll be okay. You'll remember. You've been in an accident. I'm sure it'll all come back."

Jesse's eyes closed. "So tired." He struggled to open them. "Do I get a kiss goodnight, Lady Knight?"

Scarlett nodded wordlessly, her anger gone. She closed her eyes as their lips touched. The kiss was so familiar that she opened her eyes, almost surprised to see it was Jesse and not Des' face in front of her. "Goodnight… Jesse." She stumbled over the name.

Jesse smiled slightly. "Guess we'll both have to get used to it." His voice was too soft to carry to Thomas who had moved away from the bed.

"Thank you for what you said to Tom. I'm sorry I got angry with you."

"I knew what you wanted me to say. This is the best way. I don't have the memories. Just the body."

"I didn't think about that. I'm sorry." She'd been making far too many mistakes lately. At least this one hadn't cost anyone their life.

"Stay here, Lady Knight?"

She nodded. "As long as you need me."

"Good. Dreams aren't always pleasant." His eyes closed and his breathing became even.

Scarlett pressed her lips against his forehead before she sat down. She glanced over to Thomas. "He'll be okay. Jesse is a fighter."

"He doesn't know me."

"He doesn't know himself either. You'll have to get to know each other all over again." She struggled for something comforting to say. Why was it always so hard to know what to tell people? What would Alex have said? "Maybe this is a good thing."

"How can you say that?" Thomas demanded.

"Maybe he'll have forgotten what caused him to think death preferable to living and start with a clean slate." It might not have been exactly what Alex would have said, but Thomas had started to lose his gutted look.

Thomas stared at her for a long time before he spoke. "How did you get so smart for someone so young?"

"My family believes children can make important decisions if they're given all the facts." Scarlett avoided mentioning that most of those decisions had been about demons. Her family believed if your life was at risk then you should know the reason why and be part of the decision making.

They fell into silence again and Scarlett returned to her book. When Jesse woke the next time, it was well after midnight and Thomas had already left to get some sleep. Scarlett planned to stay with Jesse until three in the morning so she could face the next demon that had been sent for her before she went home to sleep.

"Scarlett."

Setting aside her book, Scarlett rose to her feet, a smile blooming as she met Jesse's dark eyes. It was the only part of him that still looked like Des. "How do you feel?" He was starting to look healthier.

"How do you manage?"

Scarlett frowned. "What do you mean?"

"Human bodies are so weak. I didn't realise how weak they are."

"We make up for it with a strong spirit."

Jesse chuckled. "Only some people do, Lady Knight." He sighed. "I can't believe how much I've slept. I never realised what a nuisance it could be."

"Do you regret it?"

"What?"

"Becoming human."

"No. It's just going to take time to get used to being trapped by the frailties of this body."

Scarlett shook her head. "There's nothing frail about your body." Her gaze was drawn to the broad shoulders and the muscular arms that had lost only some condition in the past week.

"Compared to a demon it is."

"Why did you do it? You could have lived forever as a demon."

"The reasons are too complicated."

"Simplify them."

Jesse shook his head.

She hesitated, but she really wanted to know the answer. "You owe me a question. Truthfully answered."

"And you're going to waste it on this question? Are you sure, Scarlett?"

"The truth."

Jesse fell silent. He reached out and took her hand, his gaze dropping to look at their entwined fingers. His voice was low when he spoke. "I could give you any number of reasons. I was not always a sinner. I've lived for centuries. Boredom sets in after a while. Retribution will want to live up to his name when I'm no longer bound to you and will expect to make me pay for escaping. Any of them would be a truth."

"Look at me, Jess." She waited until his dark eyes met hers. "What reason will you give me?"

Jesse smiled wryly. "Lady Knight." He fell silent. "When I was no longer bound to you, what reason would a demon have to be in your life?"

"None," Scarlett whispered.

"As a human, only you can tell me to go. As a human, I'd have the opportunity to try and change your mind if you did."

Scarlett stared at him. "You-" she shook her head. "I can't…" she ran the fingers of her free hand through her hair. "Tell me you're joking."

"Is it so terrible that I like to be with you?"

"But to give up-"

"I didn't give up anything. Think about it, Scarlett, what did I give up?" Jesse smiled when she continued to stare speechlessly at him. "Instead, I gained a whole soul. Slightly stained, but doesn't your God believe in forgiveness?"

"Tell me you didn't do it just to be with me," Scarlett pleaded.

"I gave you all my reasons. Would you have stayed a demon if you were one?"

Scarlett laughed briefly, a sharpness to the tone. "I'm a demon hunter, what do you think the chances are I'd say yes to that question?"

Jesse smiled. "Then why are you complaining that I choose to be human rather than demon?"

"I'm not complaining… I'm… I guess you could say I'm confused."

"Then don't be. Just forget I was ever a demon."

"Can you? Forget you were a demon that is."

Jesse shook his head. "No. I remember every minute of my existence."

Alex opened the door, interrupting their conversation. "We're waiting at the elevator for you." Then he was gone again.

"I wish I was well enough to be out there helping you fight the demons sent for you every night," Jesse said.

"What did you just do?"

"What?"

"Your hand." Scarlett let go of his left hand to stare at the feather imprint. "It warmed."

"I don't know."

Scarlett ran her fingers over the feather. It was still warm to the touch, warmer than the rest of his skin. It slowly cooled as she continued to touch it. "I'm sorry about the feather. I didn't know it would mark you like that."

"Forget it." He closed his hand around hers. "I guess you'd better go before your brother is back here looking for you." He tugged on her hand so she leaned closer. "Luck?"

Scarlett smiled. Some things never changed. She lightly touched her lips to Jesse's. "I'll see you later today."

"The time is going to drag while I wait for you to return. I don't feel in the least bit tired."

"One of my family will be in to keep you company."

"It's not the same. I would rather you stayed with me. Do you know how boring it is being stuck in this bed, all alone."

Scarlett opened the top drawer and pulled out a small bible, handing it to him. She smiled. "You could try reading to pass the time."

Jesse's laugh followed Scarlett as she left the room. She hurried to the elevator where her family waited for her.

"What level demon?" Scarlett asked as they entered the elevator.

Alex pressed the elevator button. "It hasn't found you yet. But it's after three so we guessed it must be time to go."

"Maybe it wants to meet up somewhere other than the car park. Word might have got back to hell that it's an unlucky place for demons. We've certainly sent enough back from there," Riley suggested.

Blake shrugged. "No point trying to figure out demon motivation. Most of them don't think exactly like humans, so it's impossible."

They stepped out of the elevator when it reached their floor. Riley was in the lead, carrying the case of swords. Alex was at the rear, Blake beside Scarlett. The corridor was empty and the car park had only a handful of cars in it. They had parked one level up again since the security cameras still hadn't been fixed on that level. The light bulbs had been replaced though so it was no longer in semi-darkness.

Scarlett checked the area. There seemed to be no demons and yet her demon mark told her different. They were nearly at the vehicle when four demons materialised in front of them. Riley handed out their swords and put the case to the side while Scarlett wondered why they hadn't attacked yet.

"What do we call you?" Blake demanded.

The largest of the demons laughed. "Pain, Anguish, Misery and I am Agony. You cannot stop us tonight. We have been told to leave the hunter. We have permission to do what we each do best on the first innocent we find who isn't a hunter. You cannot catch us." He turned away, striding from the group.

"Riley, he's yours," Blake said. Blake quickly pointed to each demon. "Alex, Scarlett and that one's mine."

"Then come and get me, hunter." The demon jumped over the side and swung himself onto the lower level.

"God go with you," Blake called as he ran towards the ramp leading down.

"I don't like how they're splitting us up," Alex said. "Forget about your demon. Stay with me, Scarlett."

"There's enough Anguish in the world. How can I let him do things that will bring more? Please, Alex. Pain is leaving. You have to follow him."

"Not without you. This is wrong. The whole set up screams wrong."

"Then I'll follow him."

"And I'll follow you." Alex smiled as Scarlett glared at him.

"You won't be able to."

Alex and Scarlett both turned to see Nathan standing several metres from them, a gun in his hand. His deep brown eyes watched them carefully, his black hair was neatly styled and he wore a fitted suit. Off to Nathan's left the rear door of a black van opened and six men stepped out.

Scarlett's heart sank. Demons were easy, a gun

impossible. She handed her sword to Alex and walked towards Nathan. Hopefully he only wanted her.

"Scarlett. No!"

"Get out of here, Alex." Scarlett didn't look back, her gaze stayed on Nathan.

"Scarlett–"

Scarlett interrupted Alex. "Run. Now!" She couldn't look to see if he'd obeyed, but the sound of rapidly retreating footsteps gave her hope.

"How sweet," Nathan mocked. "But he won't get far." He pointed to three of the men who ran after Alex. "The rest of you in the van." The other three returned to the van, one in the driver's seat.

"Call them back and I'll come willingly," Scarlett said.

Nathan laughed. "This gun says you'll come willingly. Now get in the van."

"No."

"I'll shoot."

"I know, but it's probably better than what you've got planned for me. If you shoot me now I improve my chance of dying before you can do something worse." Scarlett tried to remain calm, but the thought of what Nathan might be planning made her want to run screaming.

"I can put a lot of bullets in you before you die and each one of them will hurt."

The gleam in his eyes made it almost impossible to remain calm. The thought of Nathan hurting her brother was all that kept her there. "I bet you've got other plans in mind. Call your men back and I'll get in the van."

Nathan stared at her a moment longer before he pulled out his mobile phone and made a call. "Back to the van." He returned the phone to his pocket. "Now get in." He gestured towards the van.

"When I see your men have returned. You could have rung anyone." Scarlett watched Nathan who continued to hold the gun on her. The minutes passed in silence. Scarlett prayed for a miracle as she fought the urge to run.

"Here they come, get in the van." Nathan looked at a point behind Scarlett.

She had started turning before he spoke, having heard their footsteps. All three of them ran towards her. She faced Nathan again. "When they're all in the van. There's no need for any of them to be left behind." She wasn't about to let her family be harmed.

Nathan gestured towards the van with his gun.

"All of you in the van." The men followed the order quietly and efficiently. "Now you."

Scarlett had no other excuse she could use to postpone climbing into the van. It looked like her miracle wasn't about to appear. Each step was an effort and climbing inside the van the biggest effort of all. She sat in the seat just inside the door and watched as it was slammed shut. The front passenger door opened and Nathan climbed in. Scarlett automatically buckled her seat belt as the engine was started and the van began to move. She was completely out of ideas. Nothing in her training had prepared her for this moment. What could she do against a gun? Why had he stopped relying on the demons? Or had this always been his plan?

"Where are we going?" Scarlett asked.

"That's none of your business." Nathan gestured to the man behind Scarlett. "Deal with her."

An arm encircled her, pinning her to the seat. Another hand appeared with a needle that was jabbed in her arm. Scarlett didn't even have time to struggle, it happened so quickly. Then her vision blurred and she lost the struggle to stay alert.

Chapter Nineteen

Scarlett slowly woke. She kept her eyes tightly shut. She could sense demons somewhere nearby. Not close enough to smell them. All she could smell was a dusty, unused smell. She took inventory of herself as she lay there. Her ankles were bound, her hands tied behind her back. She could feel her mobile phone still tucked in her back pocket. She lay on her side on something soft yet lumpy, probably a mattress by the feel of it. She could hear no sounds other than her own soft breathing. She still wasn't certain if she should open her eyes, but what choice did she have? She needed to find out where she was. She opened them slightly. The bright daylight made her want to close them again.

"I know you're awake."

Scarlett turned her head so she could see Nathan. "Where am I?"

"You aren't in any position to demand answers." Nathan came to stand over her. "Thirsty yet?" He held up a bottle of water and shook it.

Scarlett didn't answer, even though the sounds of the water made her feel thirstier. She watched as Nathan carried it away from her sight and she struggled to sit up so she could see what was around her. Just about nothing. Nathan placed the water bottle on a chest of drawers as far from the bed as possible.

"Do you know what it's like to dehydrate?" He stalked towards her. "Silent treatment? Doesn't matter. It won't change anything. Now where was I? Yes, dehydration. You'll already have the early stages. Thirst. It will get worse as the minutes pass. I really wish I was going to be here to see it, but I have other things to do."

"Like what?" She wished she could have thought of something better to say. A comment that would wipe the smug expression from Nathan's face.

"Your cousin will be next. That'll hurt Allie. She should have accepted my plans for her. It was her own stupidity she was in the situation to start with. You do something stupid, you should accept the consequences."

She had once agreed with that comment. Well,

a little. But it still annoyed her hearing him say it. "Being sacrificed to a demon isn't a logical consequence for climbing into a stranger's car."

"Death is. And your death will be a replacement for hers. Have you heard how hard it is to die of dehydration? Some say it's usually only the first few days that are the most difficult. Then the hallucinations can make things easier on you. But others say they can make things worse. If you're lucky, you won't last three days, but I've got a feeling you'll probably manage ten. There won't be much in your body by then that's functioning properly. Dizziness and light-headedness will be the nicest symptoms. Muscle cramps, nausea and eventually vomiting, even if you have nothing to throw up. Difficulty breathing, seizures, chest pains. It all sounds so lovely, doesn't it?" He smiled at her mockingly. "And now I'll leave you to get on with it."

His smile sent fear through her and she fought against it, reminding herself it was from his demon enhanced smile and not his words. But the fear had been building even before he'd smiled. "Where are the demons?" She was relieved she still sounded calm.

"Outside."

Dehydration was probably the least of her

problems then. "They'll get me before the dehydration." She wasn't sure which would be worse.

Nathan laughed. "No getting out of it so easily. The entrances have been salted. So if you manage to get loose, I'd advise staying inside. There are three demons out there that are minor enough they can walk in the daylight.

She didn't think a full day had passed. She was neither hungry nor thirsty enough for that. They had to be the demons they'd faced that morning. "Three? What happened to the fourth?" When Nathan ignored her and started to stride towards the door, Scarlett laughed. "I guess someone sent him back to hell." Her satisfaction was short lived.

Nathan paused at the open door. "Goodbye, Scarlett. I can't say it's been nice knowing you, but I'm going to cherish the thought of how painful your death will be." The door closed behind him.

Scarlett sagged against the bed and ignored the urge to call after Nathan. It wouldn't be the first time she'd been alone with demons. And no matter what she said, nothing would convince him to let her go. She'd have to find her own way out of this mess. She ignored the thought that kept returning uninvited. It was an impossible situation. She couldn't let herself believe those words.

She heard a car drive away, a sinking sensation accompanying the sound. Had he left anyone other than the demons with her? There was only one way to find out. She lay on her side and struggled to draw her legs up and pull her tied arms around them. Eventually her hands were in front of her. She eyed the rope that tied her hands together and then brought it to her mouth. The rope was new and strong. Chewing through it was a slow and tedious process. Not to mention it tasted bad and made her thirstier. She spat bits of nylon onto the bed, determined to get through it. And then she was free, the rope falling uselessly to the bed. What she needed most was water.

She swung her legs over the edge of the bed and hopped to the chest of drawers. She checked the bottle of water and was relieved to see it had never been opened and there was no damage to the bottle. She had a mouthful and put the cap back on, trying to ignore how thirsty she was.

Focus. She had to focus. She looked at her ankles. Next task. Remove the ropes. Her gaze was drawn back to the water in her hand and she forced herself to place it carefully on the chest of drawers. She stared at it longer than she should, wanting to reach out and drink every last drop. But she didn't know how long it would be before she could get more.

A quick check showed her the ropes were going to be difficult to untie. She decided to search the room to see if there was anything that could help.

Other than the bed, the drawers were all that was in the room. She slid them open one at a time. There were plenty of clothes and mice had made homes in some of the drawers. She swallowed the squeal that threatened to erupt when they scurried from the drawers. She found a box of matches, once the residents had been disturbed, but nothing else that was useful. Sitting on the floor, she fumbled at the ropes, taking longer than she liked to untie them. She needed to get out of this place before dark, but there was still a lot more to do before she could leave.

Second task completed, she thought as she rubbed feeling back into her ankles. Now what? She looked out the window as she tucked the matches into her pocket. Her phone. She pulled it out and found no coverage. But at least she knew the time. It was just after one in the afternoon.

"Think," she muttered when her gaze was again drawn to the water bottle. She turned her back on it and assessed what she did have. A bottle of water, a handful of matches, her mobile phone and a small vial of holy water that she always carried on her. Not much at all.

She rubbed her wrist, warm from the demon mark. "The demons. Where are the demons?"

She tried the door. It was locked. Next she checked the window, careful not to disturb the line of salt across the ledge. The frame was nailed shut. She saw Pain, standing guard. Beyond him the land stretched out endlessly, filled with gum trees and browning grass, some of it waist high. Nothing else was visible. She was all alone in the middle of nowhere with only demons for company. Fear hit her anew and she grabbed the frame of the window to steady herself. She couldn't give into the fear. That wouldn't help her escape.

Scarlett took a deep breath. She didn't know where she was, but she couldn't go anywhere until she'd dealt with the demons. The next task had to be praying out loud. She could do that.

It took an hour of praying to get rid of one demon. Luckily it looked like the demon had been told to stay within view of her or it wouldn't have worked. Scarlett sat on the bed and took a couple of small sips from the water bottle. Her stomach grumbled, but she ignored it. Hunger wasn't as bad as thirst and she was managing to ignore it. Kind of. She placed the bottle on the chest of drawers, her fingers still wrapped around it.

Dizziness. Light-headedness. They didn't have to be dehydration. Hunger caused them too. Her fingers tightened on the bottle as her breath caught in her throat. Difficulty breathing. That was a symptom. No. She let out a shuddering breath. Not yet. Panic also caused that. And she wouldn't panic. She'd been taught better than that. She had to focus.

There were still two demons to go and neither of them were close enough. She had thirteen hours to get rid of the other two demons and find somewhere safe before the next demon or demons were called at three a.m.

She needed to get closer to the demons so her prayers would be effective. She forced shaky legs to work as she rose and looked out the window. Why hadn't she had something to eat before she went demon hunting instead of planning to eat afterwards?

Pressing her face against the dusty window so she could see most of her surroundings didn't help. She couldn't see either of the demons. She checked the room. There was nothing that could be used as an effective weapon. Looking through the dusty glass again she saw a tree limb that would make a reasonable staff. It was a little crooked on one end and the middle slightly bent, but it would do the job.

She pulled a drawer out and tipped the clothes and mice onto the floor, doing an odd sort of dance as she tried to avoid the mice that scampered frantically across the floor until they found another hiding space. A pity finding her own safety wouldn't be as easy.

Tightening her grip on the drawer she crossed the room and swung it at the glass of the window. Careful of the salt line, she knocked out the jagged shards with the corner of the drawer. She needed to have somewhere to retreat to if things were more than she could handle. Tossing the drawer onto the bed, she vaulted outside and grabbed the tree limb. Walking around the side of the house, she scanned the area.

"This better be worth it," she muttered. Alex had to be safe. And Riley and Blake. She pushed them from her mind, focusing on her surroundings.

The house was an old Queenslander on stumps about forty centimetres out of the ground, the paint long since peeled away. Then she saw him. Misery. He came at her, claws extended and Scarlett raised her staff to block, her lips already forming a prayer. The demon continued with his relentless attacks. Scarlett met each one and wished she had her sword, or any blessed weapon. Holy water would have worked just as well as having a weapon blessed by a priest, but she didn't have enough for a staff.

Then the second demon joined in and Scarlett found herself being driven away from the house. She desperately tried to manoeuvre herself back towards it, but had no luck. The other demon, Anguish, managed to cut her arm with his claws and she hissed at the pain. She kept praying and nearly shouted in relief when, with a roar, Misery burst into flames, returning to the place he came from. That left only Anguish, but Scarlett was tiring fast. The tree limb was a lot heavier than a sword.

"You don't look too good, hunter," Anguish taunted.

Scarlett forced herself to stand firm, makeshift staff held ready. She felt blood trickle down her arm. "The odds are more even now."

Anguish laughed, the sound chilling in the heat of the late afternoon. He launched himself at her and she was driven further from the house. He smiled and took a couple of steps away from her. He held her gaze for a moment before he stared at the ground.

Scarlett looked down to see the dark spots on the earth. Her mouth opened, then snapped closed. She dropped the staff and ran towards the room. She nearly made it. The moment the demon consumed the drops of her blood from the ground pain tore through her and she dropped to one knee. She made herself push through the pain and staggered to her feet again. Grabbing the window ledge, she pulled herself inside, her teeth gritted against the agony that tore through her.

Forcing herself back to the window ledge, she smoothed the salt into a continuous line before she collapsed on the dusty floorboards. A scream was torn from her and she clutched her stomach. Her demon mark burned as the power of the demon increased. A pity it wasn't enough of a power gain to banish him from the day. She crawled towards the chest of drawers and pulled the bottom one out, a sob of pain escaping. Dumping the clothes on the floor, she ignored the mouse that scurried away, pulling the vial of holy water from her jeans. She forced her hand to stay steady. There was only a few millilitres of holy water so she couldn't afford to spill them.

Taking a deep breath, she sipped from the vial, putting the lid back on before she collapsed over the drawer. Intense burning pain shot through her and she gagged, bringing up most of the water she'd drunk earlier, streaks of blood through it.

She collapsed onto her back and panted as she tried

to fight past the lingering pain. She felt drained and wanted to sleep, but she couldn't. Rolling to her side, she nearly cried when she saw the blood trail that marked her progress from the window to the drawer.

"Des, if ever I could have done with a demon to call on, it would have been now. I could really do with some help… Jesse." Her voice was barely a whisper. She closed her eyes, and took in a shuddering breath. She really hoped she wasn't the only reason Des had chosen to become human.

Chapter Twenty

Opening her eyes, Scarlett forced herself to sit up. There would be no help. No one knew where she was. She didn't even know where she was. She was on her own. Her body shook with the exertion. Looking at the time on her phone, she groaned. Nearly five o'clock. About two hours until sunset. Then she'd be alone in the dark with a demon. She had to get rid of him before then.

First she had to make sure he couldn't get more of her blood. Looking through the clothes, she found the cleanest one and used it to bind her arm tightly. She tried not to think about the dust and mouse droppings she'd shaken from it. Then she tore off a piece of a shirt and dampened it with her precious water, using it to clean the blood droplets she'd left on the wooden floor. Looking out the window, she searched for more blood. There was none. Relieved, she sagged against the window frame. There was no time to rest.

Straightening, she saw Anguish standing far enough back that prayers wouldn't help. She'd have to go out there again. Throwing the rag in the drawer, that contained the rest of her blood, she took a mouthful of water and climbed carefully outside. Her staff was on the ground past the demon. That wouldn't help her. She warily moved along the wall of the house. Anguish continued to watch her. She came to another window and peered inside. It was a lounge room. A dusty couch that was now a rodent motel sat along one wall, a broken coffee table in front of it. A cabinet sat along the opposite wall. Sitting on it was a bowl, filled with fake fruit and covered in dust.

She tried the window. It didn't budge. Picking up a rock, she tossed it at the glass and quickly grabbed another to remove the last of the shards. A glance at Anguish showed he hadn't moved. Why hadn't he moved? What was he planning?

She didn't know and couldn't wait around to find out. She had to come up with her own plan. Climbing in the window, she avoided the broken glass on the floor, then leaned against the wall to catch her breath. Her body was still shaky from the earlier pain.

Scarlett wandered through the house until she found the kitchen. Going straight to the sink, she turned on the tap. A shudder went through the pipes and a couple of drops of rusty water landed in the stained sink before the pipes shuddered again. Scarlett automatically turned off the tap and surveyed the kitchen. There was no furniture in here. The linoleum was brittle and lifted in the corners, the cupboard doors hung open and a couple were missing. She opened drawers and looked through cupboards.

She found a handful of cutlery, some broken crockery, a partly rusted tin that had leaked some of its contents, a bag of salt that was new enough to have been left by Nathan and a bone handled carving knife with a dull edge.

She took the knife to the sink and dribbled some of the holy water over the blade. Picking up the half full bag of salt she went looking for the room she'd been locked in. The key was in the lock and she turned it, letting the door swing open. Picking up the bottle of water she had another mouthful before she checked her phone again. Still no coverage. And it was nearly five-thirty. Time was running out. She had to move faster.

Running back to the kitchen she tried the back door. It swung open with a groan of protest. Seeing there was no handle on the outside, Scarlett put the rusted tin in front of the door to keep it open. The bag of salt in one hand, the knife in the other, she walked down the two steps and rushed around to the other side of the house. Scarlett froze when she noticed Anguish had come closer. She quickly poured a salt circle on the ground, about two metres in diameter, and dropped the bag of salt in the middle. She grimaced at the circle of salt that surrounded her. Sometimes you had to use whatever was at hand, regardless of personal feelings. Salt was used by summoners, not hunters. She thought of Blake. Well, not most hunters. She straightened and her gaze sought out Anguish.

Ignoring the tremble of exhaustion that threatened to make her limbs collapse, she strode towards him, reluctant to leave the salt circle. Hopefully she wouldn't need to retreat to it. "Go home, demon and save yourself some pain."

"You will be the one to feel the pain, hunter." Anguish laughed as Scarlett held her knife in front of her. "You might as well hold a toothpick."

"Come and see what I can do with my toothpick."

The demon threw himself at her and she whirled away, striking with the knife as she did, only years of practice keeping her going. She grinned at the hiss of pain from him. Beckoning him forward with her left hand, she kept the right ready to strike with the knife.

"Didn't feel so good, did it demon?" Scarlett struck again as the demon attacked and jumped out of the way at the last second. "Let's see if we can make that holy water in your system really burn." She started to pray and had to leap out of the way as the demon attacked her with a bellow of rage and pain.

If the demon lasted too long, Scarlett didn't know how she'd keep her body going. Hunger, thirst, exertion and pain were not a good mix. She stumbled and the demon's claws caught her right shoulder. She hissed at the pain, but kept praying. She stood, half out of breath, each word an effort as she faced the demon and waited for his next move.

He threw himself at her, his arms outstretched. She tried to twist out of the way, but she wasn't quick enough and the steel arms bound her in place. They squeezed as she fought to continue her prayer. There was a flash of light, a burning pain swamped her body and the arms around her dissolved. She collapsed onto the ground her hand still clutching the knife.

She lay there, unable to move as her breath came in gasps. Her eyes closed as a wave of exhaustion washed over her. She had to move, but her limbs didn't want to obey. Her eyes opened and she noticed how low the sun was. Even that wasn't enough to make her move. She felt blood, from the cut on her shoulder, trickle towards the earth. That did make her move. Sitting up wearily, she wiped at it with her hand, then cleaned her hand on the front of her black singlet. She looked on the ground and saw one dark spot. Scooping it up she staggered to her feet. Dizziness hit her and she swayed on the spot until she could bring herself to move. Every step towards the house was an effort. Only her will kept each foot moving. She knew the window would be beyond her so she went the long way round through the kitchen.

Once she was in the bedroom again, she wiped the blood and dirt on another rag and dropped it in the drawer. Picking up the bottle of water, she forced herself to stop at one mouthful. It was hard when that mouthful did very little to quench the thirst that raged through her. Checking the cut on her shoulder she grimaced when she realised it would need to be bound. Gingerly she searched for another piece of clothing and bound her shoulder, forcing from her mind how many germs inhabited the rag. It was better than leaving blood for demons to consume. A million times better.

Scarlett picked up the drawer and the bottle of water before heading outside. She quickly built a small fire in a dusty part of the yard using broken slats from under the house, and when it was large enough, added the drawer with her blood. She wasn't going to leave it lying around for other demons. She checked the time on her phone. About fifteen minutes until dark. It had taken far too long to fight the demon and clean up.

Scarlett looked around, uncertain which direction would take her to civilisation the quickest. "I really could have used co-ordinates right about now, Des," she muttered, her voice little more than a croak. "Jesse." She sighed. It was still hard to remember to call him Jesse all the time. She looked around again. Every direction seemed the same. She took another mouthful of water and looked at the level in the bottle. Half full. She hunted outside the house until she found a tap. Nothing came out of it. More searching revealed a corrugated iron water tank on a stand, partly rusted out. There'd be no water here. Not unless it rained and the clear skies indicated that was unlikely. Swaying on her feet, she continued to stare at the sky, the light rapidly fading. She had to move.

It took long moments for her body to obey, before she could stumble over to the fire. Once she was satisfied her blood was burned beyond demon use, she spread it out so it'd die down quicker and kicked dirt over some of the embers. She wished she had water to put it out fully, but she didn't. Nor did she have the time to stand around and watch it. The last of the daylight was disappearing.

She grabbed the nearly empty bag of salt, glanced at the water bottle and knife in her hands, thought of the mobile phone, holy water and matches in her pockets and wondered how she was going to manage with so few items. She had to decide on a direction before it was too dark to choose. Moving away from the house she walked the perimeter. There were three tracks leading from the area. She didn't know which one to use. They all looked to be in similar condition. Each showed signs of recent use with tyre marks cutting through the long grass.

She sighed and chose the one leading away from the front of the house. The last of the light faded as she started to walk along the track. The moon was nowhere to be seen and Scarlett hoped it wasn't a new moon. She had better than average eyesight in the dark, but even she couldn't see on a pitch-black night. She forced her feet to follow the ruts in the dirt, one foot in front of the other. Stumbling, she barely managed to catch her balance in time. She didn't think she could've risen if she'd landed on the ground.

Pressing her hand against her stomach she tried to ignore the hollow feeling from hunger. She swallowed, her mouth dry, and had another mouthful of water. Moving forward, she lost track of time as she plodded along until she noticed the grass that had been bent over in the middle of the two ruts, suddenly standing upright ahead of her. No vehicle had gone beyond here recently. She looked around and saw the broken grass and tyre tracks where a vehicle had turned around and gone back along the track towards the house.

She breathed in deep and forced herself to turn back the way she had come. Despair threatened to swamp her. She refused to give in. Her body wanted her to drop to the ground and curl up, never to move again. She forced it to co-operate. The time on her phone said it was nine-thirty when she arrived back at the house and had another mouthful of water. Five and a half hours until more demons were sent after her. She closed her eyes and swayed on her feet. She wanted to rest. Even ten minutes, but she knew those ten minutes would rapidly become hours.

Since she was at the house, she checked the fire and was relieved to see it had completely burned out. Her fingers went to her cross. "God help me. I don't think I can go much further."

She staggered to the house and leaned against the wall. Her arms hung limply at her sides, dropping the water bottle, salt and knife to the ground. Her eyes closed and her body trembled. She knew she had to keep moving, but she was so tired. Beyond tired. Beyond exhausted. She didn't know how her body had kept going this long.

Opening her eyes, she looked at the items at her feet. She had to find another way to carry them. The salt could stay. Her mind sluggishly discarded ideas until she settled on a suitable one. Staggering inside the house, she returned to the room and tore up another garment. She used the strips to tie the knife and water bottle to the belt loops in her jeans.

She forced herself to the next track. Exhaustion dragged at her and she tried to pray for strength. Fear skittered through her when she could think of no words. Never before had she been at a loss for words to pray. Relief washed over her as the Lord's Prayer came to mind, each word accompanied by another step forward. She had barely gone twenty metres when she heard the sound of a vehicle. She looked around. Lights bounced along the third track. Scarlett moved off the track she was on in the direction of the lights. Then froze. Light didn't mean rescue. She crouched in the long grass, glad to take a break, no matter the reason. Her body trembled even harder and she relented and lay in the grass. What did it matter? She probably couldn't get up from a crouch either.

She heard the engine stop and doors open. There was silence. She waited. Then she heard cursing and recognised Nathan's voice. Her hands tightened into fists and adrenaline rushed through her. She wanted to run blindly from her hiding place. She forced her limbs to relax slightly and came up in a crouch.

"Spread out! She can't be far," Nathan ordered.

Scarlett watched as six men, highlighted by the headlights, headed in different directions. She dropped to her hands and knees so she was below the top of the grass. She began to crawl towards the track Nathan had driven along. Rocks and sticks dug into her knees and palms. She ignored them. Something scurried through the grass in front of her and she smothered the shriek that nearly escaped.

"It didn't slither," she whispered. "It didn't slither."

She took a deep breath and forced herself forward. She froze as a beam of light wandered across the grass in front of her and pressed her body against the dirt. The light meandered around the area and then moved on. Taking another shaky breath, she got back on her hands and knees, slowly crawling forward as her heart beat rapidly and her mouth felt drier than ever.

She started to pray under her breath again. A tear trickled down her cheek and she wiped it away. She refused to give in to more. Seeing the ruts of the track ahead of her, she shrunk back from them. They were too exposed. She turned in the direction they headed and continued to crawl through the long grass. She froze when she heard Nathan's voice ring out in the still night.

"Back to the van. We'll be able to track her at three. Can you hear me, Scarlett? You can't escape. Did you think you could get rid of all the demons and I wouldn't know? You'll be mine again soon. I've got handcuffs this time. Think you can get out of them?"

Chapter Twenty-One

Scarlett forced her body to stay still until the urge to run was again under control. Then she crawled forward. Minutes passed, she didn't know how many. She sat up and looked towards the house. She could barely see a metre in front of her, but the house stood out clearly with the lights of the van shining on it. She rose to her feet, certain they couldn't see her now. She stumbled onto the track and forced her legs to take larger steps. Running was beyond her.

Her fingers touched her demon mark and she whispered, "Des, I could really have used a demon who could track me down right now." She paused, then corrected herself. "Jesse." And who would be there to help him learn how to survive as a human. Would her family? "I hope it wasn't just for me you became human. Looks like you might have wasted your time." She stumbled in a rut, landing on the ground, a rock jabbing into her palm. She checked to make sure the skin was unbroken and breathed a sigh of relief. Pushing herself back to her feet, she forced herself forward, untying the bottle as she walked and taking another mouthful. She was tempted to drink it all, but she didn't. That'd be the same as admitting defeat. Until Nathan had her, she wasn't beaten. She looked over her shoulder, the house no longer visible, only a faint glow of light in the distance showing where it was. She frowned and wondered how much time had passed.

Tying the bottle to her jeans, she pulled out her mobile phone, gasping in shock. One hour and fifty-two minutes until three. And still no coverage. Pushing the phone into her pocket, she forced her legs to move quicker. Her breath came fast and she had to consciously slow it down. She didn't want to hyperventilate.

Hearing the sound of an engine in the distance, she frowned. Not a car. A motorbike? She froze. What if it was one of Nathan's men? She had no energy left to run. Seeing the single light bob towards her, fear and regret hit her. There was so much she hadn't done. So many things she wanted to say to so many people.

She wrapped her fingers around her demon mark. She'd always known a short life was a possibility.

"Gran…" she guessed there was nothing she had to tell her, Gran knew how she felt, often before she did. "Jesse…" Scarlett gasped at the sudden flair of heat that raced through her demon mark. She stared at the motorbike coming towards her. A demon? She frowned. That couldn't be right.

The motorbike pulled up beside her and she looked at the leather jacket, dark jeans and motorbike boots, the combination so familiar. The helmet came off and Scarlett stared. "Jesse?"

He grinned and handed her his helmet.

She automatically took it. "You're meant to be in hospital."

"How can I lay about when you're calling me?"

"What?"

He pulled off his left glove and held out his hand. Scarlett touched the feather imprint. It burned to the touch. "I checked myself out at five o'clock this afternoon. My father wasn't impressed. He took me home and I found out this was my method of transport." He patted the road-trail bike affectionately. "A good thing too. You can take a lot of shortcuts on a motorbike."

"I could have sworn you were human, yet now I can feel demon."

"It was the feather. It's dormant unless it's called on.

I accidentally called on it when I wished I was healed enough to be out of the hospital and helping you. You called on it when you summoned me. I think if I chose, I could become a demon again, but I don't think I could ever return to being a human if I did."

Scarlett tentatively touched the feather. It was still hot beneath her fingers. "Will you? Become a demon that is?"

Jesse shook his head. "No. I'll remain human. I think if I used it for anything major it'd cause me to turn into a demon. I was lucky I was almost recovered when I used it to finish healing." He pulled his glove back on. "Hop on, Scarlett. We need to get out of here before three a.m."

She pulled the helmet on and forced her limbs to cooperate so she could climb on behind him. Wrapping her arms around his waist, she leaned against his back. A shudder of relief went through her and some of the trembling in her body subsided as she relaxed slightly.

Jesse covered her hands with his momentarily. "Hold on tight. We've got a lot of ground to cover."

She wanted to protest when he took his hand from hers, but knew he needed both of them. He slowly turned the bike in the direction he had come from and they were off. Scarlett clung on tighter as they flew over the ground. She closed her eyes, not wanting to see how fast they went. With her eyes closed, each bump felt more jarring, and then suddenly the ride was smoother and Scarlett opened her eyes. They'd reached the highway.

It was half past two when they stopped at a service station for fuel. Jesse left Scarlett in the shadows near the curb before he rode to the bowsers. She pulled her phone out and was relieved to see she had coverage. Ignoring all the messages, she rang Blake.

"Where are you? We'll come and get you."

"I'm with Jesse."

"How'd he find you? We went up there yesterday afternoon and they told us he'd checked himself out. His father didn't know where he was, just that he took off on his motorbike. What's going on, Scarlett?"

"Never mind. I'll tell you later. Nathan swore he'd track me down. He has six men with him and they've got guns."

"Okay, let me think. Can I ring you back in five?"

"Yeah."

"Thanks. And Scarlett? How are you?"

"I'll live."

"Good."

The phone went dead and Scarlett looked up to

see Jesse wheel his bike over to where she stood. He kicked the stand down and turned to her with a packet of macadamia nuts and a bottle of water.

Scarlett dropped wearily to the ground and Jesse sat beside her. He opened the water bottle and waited for her to take it. After she had a few mouthfuls, he handed her the open packet of nuts.

"They didn't have much choice in there. I thought chocolate might be too rich for you." Jesse rubbed at a smudge of dirt on her cheek. He closed his eyes and took a deep breath before opening them to stare at her. "Do you know how I felt when you called for me? I was so close to becoming a demon to get to you quicker."

"Don't ever do that. If you become a demon never let it be because you think I need saving. I don't want that sacrifice from you."

"I know. That's all that stopped me." He pulled her against him, his arms tightening around her. "Don't do that to me again. I don't think this frail body could handle the shock."

Scarlett smiled as she felt the strength that held her. "I bet this body lifts weights."

Jesse chuckled. "Unless the weights in my bedroom are for show, I'd say you're right. But it's still frail after what I'm accustomed to."

Scarlett's phone rang and she reluctantly pulled away from Jesse to answer it. "Yeah?"

"We'll meet you at Uncle Leo's place."

Scarlett groaned. "Isn't there anywhere closer?"

Before Blake had a chance to answer, Jesse took the phone from her. "How far do you expect her to travel?" As Jesse listened, he draped an arm around her and pulled her close. "Impossible… don't try and tell me her life's in danger, you weren't there… you can't see her so forget it… no. She won't last that long on a motorbike."

Scarlett tried to pull away, "Jesse-"

Jesse shook his head and pressed hers back against his shoulder. "Good. I'll meet you there. And bring her a change of clothes and a first aid kit… I don't know, but the rags she's using as bandages are soaked through in places… okay." Jesse ended the call and handed the phone back to Scarlett.

"The cuts aren't that bad," she murmured.

"Think you're up to going a bit further?"

Scarlett sighed. "Think you can help me up?"

Jesse rose and pulled Scarlett to her feet. She swayed and he held her close. He leaned back so he could look at her. "Not much further and then you can sleep."

Scarlett nodded. Talking seemed to be too much of

an effort. She let Jesse put the helmet back on her and watched as he swung his leg over the bike and started it. He patted the seat behind him and she wearily climbed on. Her limbs were like lead.

Time felt suspended and she dozed on and off as she continued to cling to Jesse. She knew she should be worried about not being able to stay awake and coming off the bike, but exhaustion was the only sensation she could focus on.

Scarlett was brought back to her surroundings when the motorbike stopped and Jesse put his hand over hers where they were clasped at his waist. She looked around at a roadside stop and Blake's four-wheel-drive beside them. The doors opened and her brother and cousins poured out, crowding around her to help her off the bike.

Her helmet was removed and then she was pressed against Alex's chest. Her eyes closed tight as she tried to hold back tears of relief. She didn't want to freak her family out by breaking down.

"I thought one of us could have got back in time to follow the van. We were too slow," Alex said.

"Let her sit before she falls down," Jesse said.

Alex left an arm around her as he guided her to the vehicle. She looked back as Jesse was about to put his helmet on. She pulled away from Alex.

"Jesse?"

Jesse was at her side instantly. "Your family will take care of you."

Riley put his hand on the helmet Jesse held. "Stay with her."

"You can ride a bike?" At Riley's nod, Jesse let go of the helmet.

Riley pulled on the helmet and took the leather jacket Jesse handed him. It was a little large on him. "I'll meet you at Uncle Leo's place." He grinned as he started the motorbike.

Blake shook his head at how fast Riley took off. "Both Mum and Gran made him promise not to buy a bike until he's twenty-five. They ganged up on him when he was sixteen. He's regretted caving in for years now, but they won't release him from his promise. They tried to make him promise not to ride one until then either, but they were never successful."

Alex climbed into the driver's seat. "Come on, let's get out of here. It's just gone three. If we're lucky, we'll be able to get to Uncle Leo's before a demon tracks us down and leads Nathan to us."

Blake opened his mouth to say something and then with a shake of his head and an amused smile at Alex, he changed his mind and climbed into the back of the vehicle. Jesse helped Scarlett in then climbed in beside her. The moment everyone was buckled, Alex pulled out onto the highway.

Blake rummaged around in the backpack on the floor at his feet and pulled out a snaplock bag with a wet washer in it. "Not much, but it might make you feel a little better."

Scarlett pulled the washer from the bag and wiped at her face. She looked over at Jesse when he took it from her. Smiling at her, he gently wiped the smudges of dirt from her face and neck. Then he did the same for her hands. Blake unwrapped the makeshift bandage on her left arm while Jesse unwrapped the one on her shoulder. Irritation built in her at all the attention.

She pushed their hands away. "I'm not an invalid." Irritation mingled with her exhaustion.

"Never said you were." Blake dabbed at the cut on her arm with a cotton wool ball soaked in antiseptic.

She hissed. "Enough. I'll take care of it." She tried to grab the cotton wool ball, but the effort was too much.

Blake had no trouble holding it out of reach. "You're such a baby at times."

Scarlett glared at him then rounded on Jesse as he cleaned the cut on her shoulder. He smiled at her and quickly finished cleaning and bandaging it. She ignored Blake as he did the same for her arm.

"Want me to kiss it better?" Jesse asked.

Scarlett tried not to smile. And she almost managed. She ignored Jesse's soft laughter and turned towards Blake who rummaged in the backpack again. Scarlett took the wide-mouthed thermos and spoon he handed her. She stared at the thermos as fatigue swamped her further. She didn't even protest when Jesse took it from her and opened it. The smell of Gran's soup filled the vehicle. Her stomach grumbled and her mouth began to water.

"You going to feed yourself or do I need to feed you?"

Scarlett met Jesse's dark eyes and dipped the spoon into the soup. The first mouthful caused her to close her eyes so she could savour the warmth and flavours. She managed another four mouthfuls before her arm would no longer obey. "Later," she murmured.

Jesse took the spoon. "Now."

It was easier to open her mouth and accept the spoonful rather than argue. She managed half the soup before she shook her head and closed her eyes again. She felt Jesse's arm slide around her and pull her close. Her head rested against his shoulder. The last she recalled before she drifted off to sleep was Blake's voice, a hard edge to it.

"You want to explain how you knew where to find Scarlett?"

Chapter Twenty-Two

Everything came rushing back to Scarlett the moment she woke. Except she was confused for a few seconds when she opened her eyes to find she lay on a bed and stared at a ceiling instead of still being in Blake's four-wheel-drive. She turned her head to see Jesse sitting in a chair beside a window that had a heavy curtain drawn shut to keep out the sunlight that danced on the floor every time a breeze managed to shift it. She recognised the room as one of her uncle's guest rooms. The bed she lay on had an old blanket over the multi-coloured quilt that was always on the bed.

Jesse rose to his feet, crossing the room to sit on the edge of the bed. His knuckles brushed her cheek. "How do you feel?"

Scarlett slowly sat up. "Thirsty. Desperately needing a shower."

Jesse smiled. He reached for a bottle of water that sat on the bedside drawers, opened it and handed it to her. "Do you want something to eat first or a shower?"

Scarlett swallowed a mouthful of water. Then several more as it dawned on her that she didn't need to conserve this bottle. "Shower. Then I need to know what's happened while I slept."

"You didn't miss much. Your brother drives like a lunatic, which I'm surprised didn't wake you."

Scarlett laughed. "He always does when there are demons after us. I guess I must be used to it. Dad taught him how to drive, so I've had a lifetime of it. You haven't sat with me the whole time I slept, have you?"

"No, your brother was here earlier. I knew if I took the second watch you were more likely to wake up. They want me to tell them as soon as you're awake."

"I need a shower before I can face anyone." She needed to get rid of the feeling of having been locked in a rodent infested house.

"There are clothes in the guest bathroom for you. You might want to head there while I tell everyone you're awake."

Scarlett nodded. She nearly reached the door when Jesse called her name. She turned to watch him cross the room. He stood close enough for her to feel the heat of his body. She waited for him to speak. Instead, he wrapped his arms around her and pulled her close. His lips met hers. Her arms automatically slid around his neck and she clung to him. Eventually he pressed her head against his chest, his heart racing loudly in her ears. Then he drew away from her and his fingers entwined in hers.

"Next time you're in trouble, call for me sooner." He let go of her hands and held the door open for her.

Scarlett stared at him a moment before she fled to the bathroom, her feelings and thoughts a confusing tangle.

When she returned to the guest room after her shower, Scarlett paused in the doorway. Jesse reclined on her bed, the old blanket pushed to the side. Blake sat in the chair and Allie leaned against him. Riley had pulled back the curtain and was staring outside and Alex paused in his pacing when he saw her. He strode to her side and hugged her tight.

"Don't ever do that to me again."

"I can't breathe," Scarlett protested.

Alex relaxed his grip. "Do you know how I felt when I came back to find you gone?"

Scarlett pulled away. "I survived. Now tell me what happened. And when did Allie get here?"

Alex muttered under his breath and went back to pacing.

"I got a lift out here with one of your rellies," Allie said.

Scarlett nodded, but that hadn't answered her other question. "Blake?" Scarlett looked towards her cousin.

"I think he realised it was a trap. We had people stationed out near the turn off, but he didn't come that close. His sense of self preservation is amazing."

"Does his knowing about this place compromise it?" Scarlett asked.

"I hope not," Allie said. "It's cool your family has their own retreat to go relax at." She nudged Blake. "Why didn't you tell me about this place before now?"

Blake gave Allie a fleeting smile. "Because I knew you'd try and talk me into bringing you here for a weekend and it's not that type of retreat." He turned to Scarlett. "I doubt very much Nathan will tell anyone."

Riley turned from the window. "I don't believe he's that clear headed. He's completely focused on revenge. He'll have scenarios in his mind that he'll be trying to make happen. I don't think he's going to be very flexible in the way he carries them out. He needs them to go a certain way to derive satisfaction from them."

"So I'm still the target?"

Riley nodded. "Afraid so, Scarlett."

"I'm sorry. If I hadn't got in his car, none of this would have happened," Allie said.

"It's not your fault." Scarlett paused. "What's the new demon like?"

"Try nine new demons," a deep voice, from behind Scarlett, said.

Scarlett turned with a smile. "Uncle Leo."

The man, in his early forties, was large. In both height and breadth. He wore a faded flannelette shirt, jeans and his beard had a touch of grey in amongst the brown. His smile reached his blue eyes and laughter lines radiated out from them. Unlike the rest of his face, the top of his head was shaved.

"How are you, Scarlett girl?"

"Ready to hunt."

"That's good. Those demons are wearing a track around my property. It's nice to know the land doesn't need to be blessed again yet, but they're spooking the horses. I think there might have been another two, but when daylight arrived we could only see the nine. You lot must be pretty troublesome to warrant nine low level demons and two higher ones."

Scarlett laughed. "We do our best, Uncle."

"You get ready, Scarlett girl. I'll go round up the boys. Can't get those demons to stand still. I'm thinking if they catch sight of your pretty face, they'll stick around long enough for us to send them home." Leo clapped her on the shoulder before he strode down the hallway.

Scarlett turned back towards the bedroom. "Where's my sword?"

"Scarlett-" Alex began.

"My sword?" Scarlett interrupted.

"And you lot reckon I'm stubborn," Allie muttered.

Alex sighed heavily. "The swords are in our room. I'll get them if you let Blake tend your wounds."

Scarlett frowned. "I don't-"

Jesse laughed as he swung his feet off the bed. "Didn't you complain I was a terrible patient? I guess it takes one to know one. The wound on your shoulder's bleeding again. At least make sure no demon can get your blood."

Scarlett looked at her shoulder in surprise. "Fine."

By the time Scarlett had let Blake bandage both her wounds and eaten the light meal he put in front of her, it was late afternoon. Leo and 'the boys', as

Leo called his two younger brothers, waited by the two vehicles at the front of the low set brick house. Scarlett paused on the verandah that went the perimeter of the house.

She felt like she should apologise for bringing her troubles to their door. She knew the three of them were semi-retired from demon hunting. Now they bred horses and took care of any of the family who needed a break from demon hunting. Bringing demons with you wasn't considered good manners.

"Come on, Scarlett girl. Daylight's wasting," Leo called out.

Alex, Blake and Allie were already in Blake's vehicle, Riley in their uncle's. Jesse was the only one who stood beside her. With a nod, Scarlett stepped off the verandah. As she reached the vehicles, Saul and Adam came forward and took turns at folding her into their embrace. They were both as large as their brother. Adam, the youngest, was a couple of inches taller than his brother. Both had receding brown hair, Saul had the same blue eyes as Leo and Adam's were hazel. Both grinned at Scarlett as they greeted her and Saul ruffled her hair and patted her cheek.

"Good to see you Scarlett," Saul said. "No need to bring an entourage with you though."

"I hear they're more like unwanted fans," Adam teased.

"Ahh, the pain of being famous." Saul sighed theatrically and shook his head.

"Get in the ute you clowns," Leo bellowed.

Scarlett couldn't resist returning their grins. "Guess we should teach them the error of their ways." She staggered as Adam clapped her on the back. She was relieved Saul strode towards the ute without clapping her on the back like the three of them had a habit of doing.

"That's my girl. And your mate Nathan even got the numbers right and sent a demon for each of us." Adam glanced at Jesse. "That's if your young man's willing to fight with us."

Jesse nodded. "If you've got a weapon I can use. I haven't got my sword with me."

"It's in my bedroom at our new place," Scarlett said.

"Ever used a bow?" Adam asked.

Jesse smiled wryly. "I'll say yes."

"Arrows have been dipped in holy water. Makes a nice surprise." Adam glanced back towards Leo who called his name again. "Guess we'd better move before Leo has a coronary." He strode towards the ute. "Save it for the demons, Leo. You're going to blow a valve if you keep that up. Patience is a virtue brother." He tried unsuccessfully for a saintly expression.

"You want to explain what you meant when you were asked if you'd used a bow?" Scarlett clambered into Blake's four-wheel-drive. He was in the driver's seat, Alex beside him in the front. Scarlett grinned at her brother and looked pointedly at the driver's seat. Alex shrugged philosophically. She turned back to Jesse. "Well?"

"I wouldn't have a clue what this body's done. As a demon I've used many weapons and done many things. I just have to find out if this body's capable of doing what my mind knows how to do."

Scarlett grabbed the seat in front of her when she was jarred by the four-wheel-drive hitting a washed out part of the track they followed. She looked out the window before she asked Blake, "Where are we going? This doesn't lead to the main entrance."

"There's a flat clearing at the rear of the property that's only half on blessed land, making the other half accessible to demons. Uncle Leo said it's the best place to meet the demons. The set up makes it easy to retreat if we need to," Blake said.

Within minutes of arriving at their destination, demons began to appear. Adam, a sword belted to sit low on his hips, handed Jesse a bow and quiver.

"Thanks." Jesse slung the quiver onto his back.

"You've only got two dozen arrows. Better make them count," Adam said.

Jesse nodded, an arrow in his right hand, the bow clasped in his left. "And when I'm out of arrows?"

"Pray." Adam grinned before he returned to his brothers' sides.

Leo buckled on his sword, his gaze on Jesse. "Stay on my property. Shoot any demon that seems to be getting the upper hand. I'll take two demons."

"Two!" Saul punched his brother lightly in the arm. "Why should you get all the fun?"

"I'll toss you for it." Adam threw a coin up in the air.

Saul snatched it before Adam caught it, glancing at it. "Tails. I win."

"You didn't call," Adam protested.

"Yeah, I did."

"It doesn't count after you've looked at it." Adam grabbed his coin back.

Scarlett smiled as she watched her uncles. Riley wasn't the only family member who used humour to deal with the stress of demon hunting. She started to walk towards the demons and called over her shoulder, "I'll try and leave a demon for each of you, but if you don't hurry up you'll miss out."

Jesse automatically fell in beside her. Blake, Allie and Alex walked on her other side, Riley striding ahead of them. They drew their swords, almost simultaneously.

Scarlett turned to Jesse as they stopped on the boundary. "So, do you know any prayers?"

Jesse shook his head. "Not a single one. We better make sure it doesn't come to that."

Scarlett grinned at him. "I probably should teach you some if you're planning on hanging around with us. That's if you can say them." Her gaze was drawn to his left hand as she thought of his feather.

"I don't see why not, I can read a bible now."

"I still can't believe you became a human." Allie looked past Scarlett to speak to Jesse who only shrugged in answer.

"Guess we should give learning a few prayers a try." Jesse lifted the bow and put an arrow to the string, drawing it back. "Any preference on the demon you're going for?"

Scarlett gestured with her sword. "The tall skinny one that looks like it has ram horns."

Jesse aimed and let the arrow fly. The demon Scarlett had indicated bellowed with rage. Before the hunters had a chance to attack, Jesse had hit three more demons with arrows.

Adam leapt forward and attacked one of the demons. "Nice work, Jesse. You're not half bad with that bow after all."

"Enough talk." Leo swung his sword at a demon, who had materialised a sword to meet his attack. "This lot look like they need serenading." He began to sing 'The Lord is my Shepherd' and his brothers instantly joined him.

Scarlett laughed as adrenaline rushed through her and made her forget the bruises and aches she had gained in the last couple of days. She had forgotten her uncles' quirk of singing prayers and psalms. She raised her voice and joined them. The ring of metal against metal the music for the hymns.

Chapter Twenty-Three

Between them they made short work of the nine demons. Jesse collected the arrows that were left behind, when the demons returned to hell, and reluctantly gave the bow and quiver to Adam.

"Thanks."

Adam grinned as he took them. "Nice work. You can fight at my side any time." He clapped Jesse on the back.

Scarlett came to stand beside Jesse. Leo stood next to Adam while Saul grabbed three water bottles out of the ute. "What about the demons you said disappeared at daybreak?"

"We'll get them at three in the morning. No point in waiting around. It's still a couple of hours before it's dark. If we wait till then we can deal with them all at once," Leo said.

Allie stood with them. "I wish I could help you

with the next hunt. I'm getting fed up with my parents and their stupid curfews."

"Give them a chance," Blake said.

Allie snorted. "Like that's going to make any difference."

Saul joined them and handed a water bottle to each of his brothers. "I suppose that's it until three a.m. Hope they don't take too long to find you. We'll want them dealt with before we go to Charlotte's wedding tomorrow."

"What?" Scarlett stared at her uncle. "Tomorrow?"

Leo chuckled. "You been a bit preoccupied, Scarlett girl?"

Scarlett shook her head. "I thought it was still a fortnight away. I haven't even bought her a present." Charlotte was a third or fourth cousin. She could never remember which.

Leo clapped her on the shoulder. "I'm sure she'll understand. You can get her something afterwards. That way you'll see what everyone else has bought and know what she still wants."

"Have done with it and shove some money in an envelope," Adam said.

"Where's the thought in that?" Leo argued.

Saul ignored his brothers who continued to argue over the merits between giving money or choosing a gift. "You bringing your young man?" He glanced at Jesse.

Scarlett nodded. At least she hoped he'd attend the wedding with her. "That won't be a problem, will it?"

Saul shook his head. "We always expect extras. You never know who'll be in town. I'll ring Charlotte's mother and let her know to set a place for him."

"I can't believe I didn't realise how close the wedding was," Scarlett muttered.

Jesse slipped his hand in hers. "You've been spending every second at the hospital. Days blur when you're stuck in that artificial environment."

"I guess."

"No need to dwell on it. Time to head back to the house. Some people may have slept the day away, but the rest of us need to get organised so we can have an early night," Leo said.

Scarlett returned Leo's grin. Having her family around her was exactly what she'd needed after being Nathan's prisoner.

* * *

Scarlett climbed out of her car, which had been recently fixed, and walked around the front to where Jesse waited on the footpath. She shook the wrinkles from her dress, wriggling her feet inside her low heels. She missed her jeans and boots.

"I'm glad you came today," Scarlett said. "I hope it hasn't been too boring."

"It was the first time I've ever been in a church. There was a lot to see."

Scarlett smiled. "Well, I hope you're not too bored while all the photos are being taken in the gardens. We'll be going to the reception straight after, but it'll take a while to get through the photos with how large my family is." She led the way to the grassed area where her family was assembling.

Scarlett stood by Jesse's side when she wasn't needed for photos and explained some of the family relationships. Those that she knew. Many of the family tried to attend weddings and funerals. It was a way to keep in touch.

"Most of these people have the surname Hunter. Is there a larger percentage of males born into your family?" Jesse asked.

Scarlett shook her head with a smile. "No. We often keep our birth name when we marry. It's not just a surname, it's our life."

"Excuse me, Scarlett."

Scarlett turned to face a woman in her thirties. She had sandy coloured hair piled on top of her head and a frown clouded her blue eyes. "Aunt Sasha, what's wrong?"

"I'm trying to find my daughter, Hope. Sometimes I can't believe she's four. They grow up so fast." Sasha slowly shook her head. "She was playing with a couple of the older children but they said she got bored and headed back to my side. She must have been distracted because she didn't end up finding me."

"I haven't seen her since that photo I was in with you and your girls," Scarlett said.

"Thanks. I'd better keep looking." Sasha walked on to the next group of people.

It soon became apparent Hope wasn't with any of the family. Everyone broke into smaller groups to look for her. Scarlett grabbed her brother as he wandered past.

"I'm going to head this way. I left my camera in the car so I might as well get it and search in that direction while I'm at it."

"You want me to come with you?" Alex asked.

Scarlett shook her head and glanced towards Jesse who was still at her side. Alex nodded in understanding before he turned away to rejoin the search.

Jesse slipped his hand in Scarlett's as they headed towards her car. "Does the child often wander off?"

Scarlett shrugged. "I wouldn't have a clue. I haven't seen her for over a year. How about we cut across the grounds. It'll take us twice as long if we follow the path." After a few minutes of walking under large shady trees Scarlett soon realised leaving the path had been a bad idea. She glanced wryly at her low heels. "I forgot how hard it is to walk across soft ground in these things." The grassed area they'd assembled on for the photos had been more compacted.

Jesse grinned, his gaze drawn to her legs. "Boots just wouldn't have had the same effect. You want to wait here while I run to the car and get the camera?"

Scarlett looked at the trees they stood under, the air cooler out of the sun. "Keep looking for Hope too. She's a miniature version of her mum."

Jesse nodded. "You'll barely notice me gone." He moved in close. "Luck?"

Scarlett grinned before she lightly kissed him and pulled away. She laughed when he tried to pull her close for another one. "Find Hope." She gave him her car keys.

"Then I will expect a proper kiss."

"We'll see." Scarlett smiled as she watched Jesse stride through the trees until he disappeared behind some plants. She turned around, searching for somewhere to sit. She grimaced at not being able to sit on the ground. She knew Gran would be annoyed with her if she sat in the dirt under the trees and ruined her dress before all the photos were taken. Looking in the direction Jesse had gone, she wondered how long he'd take.

"Well, well, well. What a surprise meeting you here."

Scarlett whirled to face Nathan, who stood near a tree, Hope pressed to his side. There was a gun in the other hand, resting against his leg. She ignored the large blue eyes of the child and focused her gaze on the man who held her. "Let her go, Nathan."

"I really don't think you're in any position to be ordering me about."

"Let her go and I'll leave here with you. There are people searching everywhere for her. I'm guessing you don't want to be interrupted."

"Like your promise last time?"

"I came willingly. I only promised to get in the van. I didn't even try to escape until you left. Would a promise not to escape while you're with me convince you to let her go?"

Nathan pushed Hope towards Scarlett and the little girl flew forward to slide her arms around her legs.

Scarlett knelt to hold the trembling body. Wrapping her arms around her tightly.

"Get rid of her," Nathan growled.

Scarlett met Hope's wide eyes. "You want your mum?" When Hope nodded she smiled and pointed in the direction she'd come from, trying to stay calm for the child. "You run as fast as you can that way. That's where your mum is. And our family. Don't stop until you find someone you know. Okay?" The little girl nodded. Scarlett dropped a kiss on her forehead and let go of her. She turned Hope in the correct direction. "Don't look back, Hope. Just run."

Hope gave Scarlett one more look, her eyes round with fear, before she glanced at Nathan. Then her little legs carried her forward as she ran in the direction Scarlett had pointed. Scarlett rose to her feet as she watched Hope disappear.

"Move it," Nathan snapped.

Scarlett walked towards him, stumbling in her heels. She kicked them off and left them to lie in the grass. She wished she had a few minutes to peel off her stockings, but she was worried Jesse would return. She was careful not to call him and knew she shouldn't even think of him. Instead, she tried to focus on Nathan. "Where are we going?"

"None of your business. Walk in that direction."

Nathan waved the gun in the direction he wanted her to go.

Scarlett was relieved to see it was away from her family and away from Jesse. There were too many children with her family to risk going in that direction. And Jesse, she didn't want to put him in a situation where he might think his only option was to turn into a demon to save her. She forced her thoughts away from Jesse again. As Scarlett reached Nathan's side, she felt warmth in her demon mark. She carefully looked at Nathan.

"Keep walking."

Scarlett walked silently and considered her options. She'd said she wouldn't try and escape while he was with her. She was beginning to have a bad feeling he might not leave her alone this time. Either that or he'd use handcuffs. She wasn't sure how she'd escape from them. But she hadn't really promised not to escape, only implied it. Did that still count as a promise?

Scarlett was glad when they reached a path, the concrete warm beneath her stockinged feet. She glanced back the way she'd come. Trees hid where she'd left her shoes. She looked at Nathan and stopped walking. He took a few more steps before he realised and turned to face her.

"You know letting a demon into your mind is a bad idea," Scarlett said.

"What do you think you're doing? Move!"

"He could easily take over your body."

"I'm in control. He does as I ask."

"You're mad if you think you can control him for long." Scarlett stared into his eyes. There was already a hint of flames in them.

"Mad? Sure, and loving every minute of it. You can't imagine the rush."

"The demon will consume you. When you're finished using him, that's when he'll start on you." Scarlett was glad she'd left her camera in the car and only hoped Jesse would think she'd returned to her family and look for her in that direction first. She really had to stop thinking about him. She didn't want to accidentally call him to her.

"You lie. He tells me you lie."

"Of course he does. Every word he's ever spoken has probably been a lie. Demons have a bad habit of never being able to tell the truth."

"Shut up! I've had enough of this. You're not going to escape this time. He tells me you're going to try."

"I said I would the moment you left me alone. I guess even a demon can tell the truth occasionally."

"You won't have a chance. Get down on your

knees. I want to see you beg before I put a bullet between your eyes. You ruined my life. You and that family of yours. But I'll enjoy teaching the rest of them. One at a time."

"I'll never kneel to you. There's only one I kneel to and that's my God."

"Enough with the religious crap," Nathan snarled. "I could always shoot your kneecaps. Then you'd have to kneel."

"Then I'd be sitting at your feet. I won't kneel before you."

"No!" Jesse screamed. He ran out of the trees and threw himself at Nathan. The gun went off. Scarlett screamed, moving forward. Jesse staggered back, clutching at his torso. He looked at the blood that stained his hands. "Run, Scarlett."

She shook her head. "Jesse," she whispered as her gaze took in the blood.

"You're next, bitch." Nathan raised the gun again.

"No!" Jesse stepped forward, his hand still pressed against his torso. "I see you brother. I see you in those eyes."

Chapter Twenty-Four

The gun faltered. Nathan struggled to keep it pointed at Jesse. He snarled in anger and frustration.

"Brother! I have first claim on your oath. This man has caused you to break oath with me who has first claim. You must make amends." Jesse swayed on his feet. Scarlett came to his side and put an arm around his waist to help him remain standing. He held up his hand with the feather imprint. "Deception, you owe me."

In the distance, she could hear a siren. "Come away, Jesse."

"When you're safe." He reached out to touch her face. Blood marked where his fingers touched. "Safe." He turned back to Nathan. "Brother! My heart must be safe. This is my heart." He drew Scarlett forward.

Tears tracked down her face and cut paths through the blood. "Jesse. We have to get you help. Please."

"Brother. I demand reparation. Equal reparation. I leave it in your hands." Jesse staggered. He would have fallen if Scarlett hadn't lowered him to the path.

"No!" Nathan screamed. His hand holding the gun shook. "I swear by the blood shed here today-" the gun went off the moment it was pressed against his head.

A demon stood as the man fell away, far shorter than Nathan had been. His wiry body was covered in a greyish skin that rippled as he moved. His fluid face continually changed his appearance by small amounts each second. "No debt is owed. An eye for an eye. A bullet for a bullet. I have given equal reparation in the only way possible."

The deep familiar voice of the demon reminded Scarlett of the first day she'd met Jesse.

"Find peace, brother," Jesse said. The demon vanished and Jesse's eyes closed.

"No! Don't die, damn you." Scarlett pressed her hand against the blood that welled from his wound.

"You would have me go to hell?" Jesse opened his eyes again.

"No. I would have you live."

"And if I shouldn't?"

"Please, Jesse. Live."

"Hell?"

"No. Never. If anyone has earned the right to heaven, it's you."

"Then bless me, don't damn me."

A shuddering sob escaped and Scarlett bit her bottom lip to try and control the urge to cry and scream and demand he be allowed to live. "I do, Jesse. I bless every day that brought you to me. Just hang in there. You have to live."

"I love you, Lady Knight." He smiled up at her and closed his eyes again.

"No. Jesse! Open your eyes. Please." She swallowed the hard lump that seemed to be lodged in her throat. She pressed down harder on his wound and tried to stem the flow. Her lips moved as she began to pray. Then hands dragged her away. She fought against them.

Alex's arms wrapped around her. "Scarlett. They're trying to save him. Let them do their job. No crying now. All will be well." Alex stroked her hair as he held her. "Nathan can't harm you again."

"Only if Jesse lives. All will be well only if he lives," Scarlett said.

"If he's meant to, then he will."

Scarlett tried to pull away, but Alex tightened his hold. "I can't accept that."

"I know. You never can. You always want to do

more. There's no inevitable, no inescapable events, only your willpower. If you could, you'd drag the world kicking and screaming into line, making it how you think it should be."

"At least it's better than walking off from a situation that looks impossible." When Alex's hand stilled in her hair, she cried out, "Oh Alex. I'm sorry. I didn't mean that."

"I understand. You're hurting. I'm convenient."

"That's no excuse–"

"Come on. Let me take you to the hospital. We'll follow the ambulance."

"I want to ride with him. I need to be there with him."

"They won't let you ride with him. Come on, Scarlett. We'll get there just behind them."

Scarlett let Alex lead her along the path. She saw how many of the family stood nearby. She hadn't noticed them before as she'd been so focused on Jesse. She took the handkerchief Blake held out to her when he and Alyssa reached her side. Staring at the white linen, she watched as it was quickly stained red from her fingers. Blake took it from her and used it to wipe her face before he pressed it into her hands again. Riley joined them and handed her shoes to her.

Scarlett looked back to where the police dealt with

Nathan. Leo, Saul and Adam stood talking to them. She paused and frowned.

"You can talk to them later." Blake dropped his arm around her shoulders to rest near Alex's arm. "The uncles will sort it out. They told me to let you know they'd make sure the blood can't be used by demons."

"Let's get you to the hospital. Everything else can be dealt with later," Alex said.

Scarlett nodded and hurried along the path. She didn't bother with her shoes. She could have walked over glass and not felt it. Her entire body felt numb. All she could feel was the blood on her hands. Even after wiping most of it off with the handkerchief she clutched.

The drive to the hospital was a blur and Scarlett couldn't have said who had driven them or which vehicle they'd taken. It wasn't until Alyssa took her to the restroom to help her clean up that she finally started to notice her surroundings.

Scarlett stared at herself in the mirror. Her gaze drawn to the blood that still streaked her cheek. Jesse's blood. She looked down at her hands and the blood that stained her dress. "This is why we always wear black. But it didn't seem right to wear black to a wedding." She looked up to meet Alyssa's gaze in the mirror.

Alyssa took the handkerchief and washed it out before she used it to clean the blood off Scarlett's face. "Guess you'll have to buy a new dress. The stains will never come out of that one."

"I don't care. I just want to find out how Jesse is." She washed the blood from her hands and watched as it swirled away.

Alyssa took a vial of holy water from her purse and tipped some of it in the sink to be washed away with the blood. "I don't know how you can remain so calm. I'd be screaming at them to let me see him." She returned the half empty vial to her purse.

Scarlett stared at Alyssa for a moment. "Training and shock."

Alyssa smiled wryly. "Shock I can relate to. Come on. You don't look so bad now. At least not bad enough to completely freak Jesse's father like you would have before."

Scarlett made her way to where her family waited for her. Thomas was with them, looking pale and shaken. She immediately went to his side and put her arms around him. He hesitated before he returned her embrace.

"I can't find anyone to ask what's going on," Thomas said.

"At least they'll talk to you. They won't tell me

anything," Scarlett complained. She stepped back. "He'll get through this. We won't let him give up."

"Blake told me what happened," Thomas said.

"I'm sorry."

"You don't have anything to be sorry for. I'm just glad that madman shot himself. It saved me the job of hunting him down."

"Tom. No! Don't talk like that."

"I'm not a Christian like you, Scarlett. Someone hurts my boy I'm not going to forgive them or let them get away with it. That man's lucky he killed himself."

Everyone turned towards the doorway as someone entered the waiting area. It was Detective Tuck. He paused and looked at each of them. His gaze fell on the bloodstained dress Scarlett wore.

"This is becoming a habit, Hunter."

Scarlett stepped closer to Tuck. "So it would seem. And it's Scarlett."

"You want to tell me what happened? From what I've been told, you were his actual target. It's difficult to believe he'd have shot himself before he'd taken care of you."

Scarlett shrugged. "Maybe he felt he'd already dealt me a killing blow."

"That doesn't add up for me," Tuck said.

Blake joined them. "Detective."

"Hunter."

"It's Blake."

Tuck smiled. "You have an aversion to your last name?"

Blake smiled. "Not at all. It's just practical to avoid it when around so many of my family."

"These two are family as well?" Tuck gestured towards Alex and Riley.

"Yes. My brother and cousin. Look, I don't know what game you're playing, but can you ask your questions so we can go back to waiting to see how Jesse is doing?"

"I find it hard to believe Nathan shot himself."

"Someone as mad as him would have had his own demons to deal with. It's easy enough to lose control of your demons and kill yourself."

Tuck stared at Blake as he assessed his words. "Is that your personal opinion or fact, Hunter?"

"I'd be tempted to call it fact. With the demons being metaphorical of course." Blake grinned fleetingly.

"Of course." Tuck nodded. "If you think of anything else, you know how to contact me."

Blake nodded.

"I don't suppose you could find out how Jesse is," Scarlett asked.

"I still have a lot to-"

Scarlett interrupted Tuck. "Please. I'm desperate to find out. The nurses and doctors seem to have disappeared." When Tuck hesitated Scarlett reached out to him. "Please."

Tuck looked at the hand on his, a few smudges of blood had been missed. He remained silent a moment longer before he gave a single nod. "I'll see what I can do."

"Thank you." Scarlett watched as Tuck disappeared. She turned to Thomas who had come to her side the moment Tuck left. "Hopefully he'll be able to find out how Jesse's doing."

Thomas nodded. "I'd hoped to be done with these bedside vigils."

"I'm sor-"

"Please stop thinking it's your fault."

"I can't help it. I keep wondering if there was something I could have done differently." Scarlett closed her eyes. "And I keep hearing the sound of the gunshot over and over again."

Before Thomas could say anything, Tuck returned to the waiting room. "He's still in surgery. They're optimistic about the outcome though. You should be able to see him in approximately an hour. He'll still be sedated, but at least you can see him."

"Thank you," Scarlett said softly.

Tuck shook his head. "Maybe I should be saying that. I have a reasonable ear for voices. They're a little different over the phone to what they are in person and I hate guessing, I much prefer concrete evidence. I know when to leave well enough alone and not to look further into a matter even when it goes completely against the grain to do so. I look forward to hearing from you again. Hunter." He turned and strode away before any of them could speak.

Blake burst out laughing. "I guess it was inevitable at some stage."

"You don't think it'll be an issue?" Scarlett asked.

Blake shook his head.

Alex spoke before Blake could say anything else. "Tom must be feeling a little confused by our conversation." He looked over to Thomas who watched them carefully. "Scarlett rang him with information about a crime, but she didn't want to risk anyone knowing it was her. Some criminals are unethical at finding out who have accused them."

"Was the call linked to what happened with Nathan?" Thomas asked.

"There was a link," Alex said.

"How did Nathan find out about her phone call?" Thomas asked.

"I don't believe he did. It was a rather complicated set of circumstances that had him trying to kill her," Alex said. "He certainly wasn't a sane man."

"I guessed that," Thomas said.

Blake checked his watch. "Why don't we get something to eat in the cafeteria while we wait? Starving ourselves won't help Jesse."

"I couldn't eat," Thomas protested.

"I'll wait here in case a doctor or nurse comes looking for you," Alex said. "At least try to have something to eat. Scarlett missed breakfast this morning. If you don't go, I know she won't."

"I did have breakfast," Scarlett protested.

"Two mouthfuls of toast doesn't count," Alex said.

Scarlett shrugged. "I was running late."

Thomas reached for Scarlett's hand. "Lunch. Jesse'll be annoyed if you get sick. You're important to him."

Scarlett reluctantly gave in and was surprised, when she sat down at a table in the cafeteria, that she ate all the food Riley put in front of her. They still managed to arrive back before the doctor came to tell them Jesse could have one visitor at a time.

"You go, Scarlett," Thomas said.

"But-"

Thomas interrupted Scarlett. "He responds more to you. I want my boy to get well. Tell him I need him too."

Scarlett's eyes watered as she threw her arms around Thomas. "Thank you." She followed the nurse, the doctor had asked to escort her to Jesse's room, while he stayed and explained Jesse's condition to Thomas. She paused in the doorway. Her breath caught as she saw him. The healthy colour he'd gained was gone and he was pale once again.

When Scarlett reached his side, taking his hand in hers, she saw the ring was missing. She found it in the drawers beside his bed. Slipping it back on, she held onto his hand tightly. "Don't leave me, Jesse. I really need you." She continued to stand beside him, unwilling to move away to bring a chair over, even though her legs ached from her long walk the other night.

"Scarlett?" Jesse looked up at her groggily.

Scarlett could only smile and reach out to run her fingers across his cheek.

"You're safe?"

Scarlett nodded, her throat tight from trying not to let tears spill.

Jesse's eyes closed and Scarlett made a sound of protest that had him opening them again.

"Don't leave me," Scarlett whispered.

Jesse smiled weakly. "You still owe me a question. I have to stick around at least long enough for you to answer it."

"What's your question?"

"I'm saving it. Never know when I might need it." Jesse yawned. "So tired. Luck?"

Scarlett grinned as tears pooled in her eyes. "Always." She leaned forward to press her lips to his.

Chapter Twenty-Five

Scarlett leaned against Jesse's back, her arms around his waist, the sound of the motorbike making it impossible to talk. She watched the houses and cars they passed and tried to figure out where they were going. She had a feeling Jesse had taken them on a meandering trip, just to keep her guessing. It now seemed like they were headed for his house. His and Thomas' house. When they pulled up in front of Thomas' shed, she hit him on the arm.

Laughing at her, he hopped off the bike.

The moment she was off the bike, and the helmet was hanging on the handlebars, Scarlett put her hands on her hips. "You sure you couldn't have gone via Townsville?"

Jesse tried to put his arms around her, but she pushed at his chest and glared at him. He continued to grin. "You wouldn't deny me a kiss when I've so recently been on my death bed?"

"Recently! Try nearly a fortnight ago and you used your demon powers to finish healing. You're going to have to stop doing that."

"Then you're going to have to stay out of danger," Jesse said.

Scarlett shook her head. "I'm a demon hunter. It goes with the territory."

"Then I'm not about to stay in bed recuperating if I can hurry up the process without becoming a demon. I'll always be at your side when you face danger."

Scarlett's glare softened. "I've been doing this for years. I can manage without you at my side."

"I know. But I like to be there anyway."

Scarlett relaxed her arm and let him pull her close. "So why did you bring me here? And don't look at me like that."

"Like what?" Jesse tried for an innocent expression.

"Dessert. Now why are we here?"

Jesse chuckled. "Well, since you can't be tempted..."

"I can't."

Jesse led her to the doors of his father's shed. It was an old timber building with two large doors at the front and dusty windows scattered along each side. Pulling out a key, he inserted it into the large padlock. He looked down at her with a smile.

"Quit with the theatrics." Scarlett pushed his hands out of the way and turned the key. She removed the padlock and swung the door open to stare in open-mouthed surprise.

Jesse stepped inside and flicked on a switch to flood the building with light. An eighteen-foot timber yacht, on a trailer, sat in the middle of the building. A thin layer of dust covered the benches that ran either side of the shed, but the boat was spotless.

"Where did it come from?" Scarlett looked between the sailing boat and Jesse.

"Dad's had it for a couple of decades. Apparently I was once a good sailor." He grinned at her.

She couldn't help worrying. He didn't have the memories, only the body. "Have you done any sailing in your past life?"

Jesse chuckled. "All manner of craft. I'm not about to capsize her."

"Capsize her? You're taking her somewhere?" She stared at the boat. She could almost feel the movement of the deck beneath her feet, nearly hear the snap of the sails as they filled with the wind. It had been so long since she'd been sailing.

Jesse took her hand. "We won't be able to sail

around Australia, but how about Moreton Bay? Will that do?"

Scarlett threw her arms around Jesse, holding him tight. "Perfect. Absolutely perfect."

Free Ebook

Subscribe to Avril's newsletter to receive a free ebook. This ebook is exclusive to those on her mailing list. To find out more about this offer visit: http://www.avrilsabine.com/free-ebook/

*

We value your privacy and will not sell, rent, exchange or loan your email address to third parties. Your information is confidential and you are under no obligation to remain on the mailing list and can unsubscribe at any time.

Acknowledgements

Thank you Mum and Cat. Once again your help has been invaluable.

To The Reader

If you enjoyed this book, why not consider leaving a review to help other readers discover it too? Reader engagement is one of the few ways that lets an author know readers want more books in a particular series or genre. So leave a review and tell friends, not only about this book but also about other ones you've enjoyed, so you can continue to enjoy books by your favourite authors for years to come.

Dreams are meant to be lived,

Avril.

About The Author

Avril is an Australian author who lives with her family on acreage in South East Queensland. She writes mostly young adult speculative fiction, but has been known to dabble in other genres. You can find more information about her at her website www.avrilsabine.com where you can also subscribe to her newsletter to be kept informed about new releases, current projects, blog posts and exclusive news.

Titles By Avril Sabine

Stories about strong characters and characters who discover their strengths.

SERIES

Assassins Of The Dead- Young Adult Fantasy/ Paranormal

Book 1: Dark Blade

Book 2: Dragon Touched

Book 3: Society Against Vampires

Book 4: King's Request

Dragon Blood- Young Adult Urban Fantasy (with elements of romance)

(5 book series)

Book 1: Pliethin

Book 2: Wyvern

Book 3: Surety

Book 4: Knight

Book 5: Mage

Dragon Mage- Young Adult Urban Fantasy (with elements of romance)

(Series two of Dragon Blood series)

Book 1: Promise

Dragon Blood Chronicles- Young Adult Urban Fantasy (with elements of romance)

(Companion stand alone series to Dragon Blood)

Book 1: Oath

Book 2: Betrayed

Guardians Of The Round Table- Young Adult Fantasy LitRPG

(Co-written with Storm and Rhys Petersen)

Book 1: Dexterity Fail

Book 2: Goblin Boots

Book 3: Singed Feathers

Book 4: Frog Mage

Book 5: Crystal Mine

Book 6: Cursed Harp

Rosie's Rangers- Young Adult Western Steampunk

(6 book series)

Book 1: Justice

Book 2: Vengeance

Book 3: Treachery

Book 4: Accused

Book 5: Wanted

Book 6: Corruption

Mark Of Kings- Children's Fantasy

(Upper middle grade/preteen)

(4 book series)

Book 1: The Arena

Book 2: The Island

Book 3: The Assassin

Book 4: The King

STAND ALONE SERIES

Demon Hunters- Young Adult Urban Fantasy/ Horror (with elements of romance)

Book 1: Blood Sacrifice

Book 2: Retribution

Book 3: Tainted

Book 4: Premonition

Book 5: Cursed

Book 6: Feud

Book 7: Extrication

Plea Of The Damned- Young Adult Urban Fantasy/Paranormal

(6 book series)

Book 1: Forgive Me Lucy

Book 2: Forgive Me Aiden

Book 3: Forgive Me Jena

Book 4: Forgive Me Kobe

Book 5: Forgive Me Marti

Book 6: Forgive Me Dawson

Realms Of The Fae- Young Adult Urban Fantasy
(with elements of romance)

The Sword (short story in Like A Girl Anthology)

Heart Of Stone

Book 1: A Debt Owed

Book 2: Marked By The Hunt

Book 3: The Magic Collector

Book 4: An Unexpected Betrayal

Book 5: Imprisoned By Iron

Fairytales Retold (Short Stories)

Snow-White And Rose-Red

The Twelve Brothers

The Light Princess

Beauty And The Beast

Sleeping Beauty

Aschenputtel

The Golden Bird

The Frog Prince

The Death Of Koshchei The Deathless

Myths And Legends Retold (Short Stories)

Ion, Son Of Apollo

Sir Gawain And The Maid With The Narrow Sleeves

Princess Ilse, The Giant's Daughter

YOUNG ADULT NOVELS

Young Adult Fantasy (with elements of romance)

Elf Sight

Earth Bound

Young Adult Urban Fantasy

Stone Warrior (with elements of romance)

The Jungle Inside

Young Adult Contemporary (with elements of romance)

Through Your Eyes

The Ugly Stepsister

Perfect Little Princess

Young Adult Contemporary/Paranormal

Whispers In The Dark (with elements of romance and same sex relationships)

Over Too Soon (with elements of romance)

Young Adult Sci-Fi

Experiment X-One-Six (Urban Sci-Fi/Superheroes)

An Endless Dawn (Post Apocalyptic Sci-Fi)

CHILDREN'S BOOKS

Dragon Lord (Preteen/early teens) (Fantasy)

The Irish Wizard (Upper middle grade) (Urban Fantasy)

SHORT STORIES

Urban Fantasy

Eternally Late

Dealings With Joe

Glimpses (short story in That Moment When Anthology)

Contemporary

The Brat Next Door

Fantasy LitRPG

(Set in the same world as Guardians Of The Round Table Series)

Tales Of Inadon 1: The Disc (Co-written with Storm and Rhys Petersen) (short story in Game On! Anthology)

Post Apocalyptic Sci-Fi

Compulsive Directive

NONFICTION

A Year Of Weekly Writing Exercises (Creative Writing)

Cooking For Families With Allergies (Cooking) (Co-written with Storm Petersen)

Tell Me A Story, Grandma (Memoir)

For the most up to date details on available titles visit:

www.avrilsabine.com/books/bibliography

Demon Hunters Series

To learn more about this series visit:

www.avrilsabine.com/series/dh

BOOKS AVAILABLE IN THE DEMON HUNTER SERIES

Book 1: Blood Sacrifice

Book 2: Retribution

Book 3: Tainted

Book 4: Premonition

Book 5: Cursed

Book 6: Feud

Book 7: Extrication

Disclaimer

This is a work of fiction. Names, characters, businesses, places, events and incidents are either the products of the author's imagination or used in a fictitious manner. Any resemblance to actual persons, living or dead, or actual events is purely coincidental. The opinions expressed or beliefs held are those of the characters and should not be assumed to be the opinions or beliefs of the author.